Wake Up, Wanda Wiley

Andrew Diamond

This is a work of fiction. Names, characters, and events are the products of the author's imagination. Any resemblance to actual persons or events is purely coincidental.

Cover design by Lindsay Heider Diamond. Illustration of reclining woman by Rosie Piter, licensed from Acclaim Images (image id 0071-0905-2723-4139). Illustration of woman typing by ingenium, courtesy of Shutterstock (image id 365303444).

ISBN-13: 978-0996350792
ISBN-10: 0996350799

DEDICATION

For Sophia Morris, who said,
"Why don't you write something funny?"

1

This new character, Hannah thought, was somewhat thickheaded. That didn't surprise her. Wanda had written quite a few like him. Obtuse alpha males with single-minded intent. This one pursued a line of questioning that had nothing to do with anything in her world. He didn't even take the time to notice how out of place he was—a twenty-first-century action hero in a late-nineteenth-century Victorian farmhouse, location Nowhere.

The furniture was worn, the floors creaked underfoot, and the rugs were going bare. There was no country outside the tall, curtained windows, no landscape beyond the few feet of grass and bushes visible through the ever-present fog. The ticking clocks inside the house had no hands. There was no time to tell.

The man asked again about the president, and again he called her Anna.

Now she put it together. He wasn't one of Wanda's characters. He belonged to Ed Parsippany. Wanda was merely ghostwriting. She obviously didn't know what to do with this guy or he wouldn't have wound up here.

"You're in the wrong book," Hannah said.

"Come again?"

"This is a romance. You're an action character."

"I'm sorry, lady, you're not making any sense."

"You're looking for the president?"

Now he was alert. He fixed her sharply in his sights. "What do you know about the president?"

"The president has been stolen."

Trevor grabbed her by the arm and whispered roughly in her ear. "How do you know that? Who briefed you?"

"No one briefed me," Hannah said, pulling her arm away. "It's the title of a book. *The President Has Been Stolen.*"

Trevor shook his head gravely. "'Fraid not. It's classified information. How did you come by it?"

Hannah let out a sigh of frustration, then said slowly, as if talking to a child, "It's a book. Wanda's ghostwriting it. She got the outline from Ed Parsippany—"

"Parsippany? You know which group he's affiliated with?"

"Random House. He just makes the outlines and then farms out the writing to other authors."

Trevor clapped his hand on her shoulder and hissed, "Is this some kind of code you're talking in? What's an outline? You mean a plan, right? You're telling me there was a plan to kidnap the president. Have you seen this plan?"

"Yes. Take your hand off me!" She pushed his hand off her shoulder and rubbed the sore spots where his fingers had dug into her flesh. "God, I never understood why all her men have to be so domineering."

"Who's this *she* you're talking about?"

"Wanda."

"Wanda," Trevor repeated thoughtfully. He rubbed his chin as if trying to recall some long-buried bit of information. "Doesn't ring a bell. Is it an acronym for some terrorist organization?"

"Wanda is the author," Hannah said.

"Of the plan to kidnap the president?"

Hannah looked him over quietly for a second. "You're handsome enough," she said. "But not my type."

"Where is the president?"

"Not my type at all. I don't like tough guys. She knows that."

"Who? Wanda?"

"Yes." The green silk of her satin dress rustled as she turned. Trevor couldn't see the worry in her eyes, the furrowed brow, or the way she wrung her hands. He scanned her top to bottom, looking for the telltale bulge of a holstered pistol beneath the dress. There didn't seem to be one, at least not from the waist up. Below the waistline, the skirt flared out wide enough to conceal a bazooka, but if she was packing anything down there, she couldn't get to it without hiking up the dress, and that would be a loud and awkward operation.

So no gun handy, Trevor thought, but she still could have a knife. A flat-handled instrument, like those throwing knives magicians use. If she had the proper training, she could draw it and slash his throat in one smooth motion. And a woman like this, as pretty as she was in that satin dress, would obviously be trained to work at close quarters. To seduce a man, get his guard down, draw him into slashing range.

Where would she keep the knife? Down around her calves or ankles, which were covered by the dress. Of course, Trevor thought. No one wears ankle-length dresses anymore. Unless they're trying to conceal something.

He stepped forward quickly while her back was turned, and in one smooth motion, he crouched and swept his hands beneath the dress, sliding them up the outsides of both legs from the ankles to the midthighs.

She spun at once and slapped him, aiming for the face, but in his low crouch, the heel of her hand caught him on the ear and knocked him sideways. "Creep!"

He sprang up immediately and grabbed her wrists. Her nostrils flared and her eyes went wide with terror.

"I don't have rape fantasies!" she pleaded.

The hard fighting glint in Trevor's eyes softened to a look of confusion. "What?"

"I'm not Lesley Fairchild."

Trevor shook his head as if trying to snap out of a bewildering dream. "Who?"

"Lesley," Hannah sniffed. "From the first series. You know, the *Taken* books. *Taken by Storm*, *Taken by Force*, *Taken in the Night*. That whole erotica series that had the feminists up in arms."

Trevor's eyes narrowed as he began to realize he was dealing with a mentally ill person. Maybe if I dip into her delusional language, he thought...

Then, tentatively, he asked, "Was the president also"— he watched her eyes for signs of panic—"taken?"

"Originally, I was the heroine of that series," Hannah said absently.

"What series?"

"The *Taken* books."

OK, Trevor thought. She's stuck in her own train of thought. Try to draw her out. "You said something about feminists?"

Hannah nodded. "They thought the series was regressive. You know, a helpless woman at the whim of a man's desire. And liking it. That was what sent them over the edge."

"These feminists…" Trevor cocked his head like a dog when it listens closely. "Were they in on the plan to take the president?"

"Let go of my wrists."

"Because feminists can be pretty angry, you know."

"That's a stereotype. Please let go of me."

"I need to see what's between your boobs."

"Excuse me?"

"You could have a knife in there. That's some pretty substantial cleavage."

"It's just the dress," Hannah said. "It smooshes my— Wait, who carries knives between their boobs?"

"Terrorists," Trevor shot back. "Spies. Kidnappers. Feminists."

"God, what an awful character!"

"Who?"

"You! No wonder Wanda hates the thriller genre."

"Who's Wanda?"

"I told you. She's the author."

"You're trying to distract me," Trevor said. "I need to inspect your cleavage."

"For knives," Hannah said in a mocking tone.

"That's right."

"And what about my butt crack? How many do you think I could sandwich in there?"

"The butt crack's not a threat," Trevor said. "Not in that dress. You'd have to unzip the back to get to it."

Hannah rolled her eyes and sighed. "Oh God!"

Trevor pushed both her wrists into his left hand to free up his right. "Now listen," he said, "if we were at base, we'd have a female officer do this."

"You'd have a woman rough me up?"

"No one is roughing you up. This is a matter of national security. I'm just going to slide one finger down there. One finger and—" He broke off abruptly and looked so strangely at her chest that Hannah, wondering what he saw, was forced to look down too.

"What?" she asked. "What's wrong?"

"Your dress," said Trevor.

"What about my dress?" She saw no stains or tears in the shiny blue fabric.

"It was green a minute ago."

"You're right," Hannah said.

"And now it's blue. How..." Trevor looked at her suspiciously, and for the first time, she saw a hint of uncertainty in his eyes. "How did you change it? I haven't taken my eyes off you since we've been in this room."

"She's revising," Hannah said.

"Who?"

"Wanda."

Trevor watched her closely as if to figure out what trick she was trying to play. "What does that mean? Revising?"

"She's rewriting the scene. Look at the window."

Trevor glanced quickly toward the window without turning his head. This woman was a clever one, and he didn't want to take his eyes off her for too long.

"The curtain's closed," he said, returning his eyes to her after the quickest of glances. "There's nothing to see." He was pleased with himself for having the presence of mind to avoid whatever trick she had attempted.

"The crack between the curtains," she said. "What do you see in the crack?"

He gave another split-second glance. "Daylight," he said with proud machismo.

"And what time was it when you came in?" she asked softly.

"I came in ten minutes ago."

"But the world you came from had clocks and time. What time was it?" She led him gently.

"It was midnight."

"And now it's daylight. How does daylight happen ten minutes after midnight?"

With an unshakable confidence, he said, "We're in Sweden."

Hannah shook her head. "We're not anywhere."

"You're either psychotic," Trevor said, "or you're a witch."

A witch, Hannah thought. *He's scared of me. He's starting to crack.*

"Do you really think I'm hiding a knife between my breasts?"

Trevor suspected the question was a trick. His eyes narrowed. "I believe you want me to believe that you do not have a knife between your breasts."

"Go ahead and check," Hannah said.

Trevor still wasn't sure what she was trying to pull. "Why do you want me to check?"

"So you'll let go of my wrists. This is ridiculous."

He thought back to his criminal psychology courses at the academy. Of course she'd try to sell the idea that checking her cleavage for a knife would benefit *him* when in fact it would benefit her. But how? Trevor began to suspect he was up against an unusually clever criminal possessed of special psychological powers. A Hannibelle Lectress, perhaps.

"Go ahead," Hannah whispered. "Just one finger though. Slide it right on down."

Trevor felt his throat going dry. "That's a"—he looked from her chest to her face and back again—"that's a lot of cleavage. Might need two fingers."

"OK," Hannah said as she pushed her chest out. "Don't cut yourself."

Trevor swallowed, a dry convulsion of the throat, then slid his index and middle fingers between her breasts, withdrawing them so quickly his hand almost hit her chin on the way out.

"Satisfied?" she asked.

"Yeah." He let go of her wrists.

"Well I'm not," she said as she turned toward the window. "I never am. Not with the stories Wanda writes for me."

Trevor was more lost than ever.

"I mean, that was the least erotic touch I've ever felt from a man." She opened the thick velvet curtains onto a world of fog. "That was like going to the dentist."

"What's out there?" Trevor asked as he approached the window.

"Nothing."

"There has to be something."

"A porch out front, and about six feet of walk. There's a strip of grass on the side of the house, and an old hand-pumped well in back."

"Where's the rest of the world?"

"It's gone missing," Hannah said. "That's what happens when you're depressed."

"Are you depressed?"

"To the extent that Wanda is, yes."

"Wanda the writer?" Trevor struggled to put the pieces together, but like a good investigator, he kept his eye on her for clues. "How long have you been in this house?"

"On and off for years," Hannah said.

"Alone? Always alone?"

She shook her head. "No. I get out now and then. Every time Wanda starts a new romance series." She stepped away from the window and the fog, toward the clarity of the lamplight. "She did the *Taken* series first, and I was the heroine of the first draft. But I didn't like hardcore erotica. I didn't like being 'taken.' I wanted to be seen and heard, so she wrote me out."

She looked to see if Trevor was still listening. He was, but the attention he gave her was more clinical than personal, like a psychiatrist evaluating a new patient in the asylum, or a cop looking for cracks in the story of an unreliable informer.

"The second series was *The Spanking Billionaire*. I like a good spanking as much as anyone, but it gets old after a while. And the billionaire was crass and obsessed with power. She could tell I didn't like him, so she wrote me out again. Raven Locksley became the heroine of that series.

"Then there was the *Kilted Brute*. The foul-mouthed Scotsman with his reeking armpits and his red-haired horse dong. The Highlands are romantic in pulp novels, but when you're there, it's cold and windy, and maybe I'm old-fashioned, but I don't like men in skirts."

She picked at her fingernails for a moment, and when she looked back up, Trevor was making an inventory of the room with his eyes, lingering on the ancient furniture and turn-of-the-century photos.

"Wanda got sick of the criticism, people saying her books were thinly veiled porn, so she cast me in a Regency. You know, early nineteenth century, Jane Austen kind of stuff. I hated it. It was so confining, having to dress like that, not being able to speak your mind. The gender roles were like straitjackets. There was no chemistry between me and Lord Gladwell, so she wrote me out again, and Eunice Birdwhistle became the lucky young miss.

"Every time she writes me out, she sends me back to this house. I sit here all alone while she swears that someday she'll get back to me. Well I don't know anymore."

Her silk dress rustled as she sat heavily on the couch. A look of weariness and despair came over her.

"The Regencies did well," she said. "The first few, anyway. She's finishing book nine of the series. You know what that means?"

Trevor watched her closely, convinced now she was insane. "What?"

"It means I've been in this house on and off through eighteen books. Three *Takens*, three *Spanking Billionaires*, three *Kilted Brutes* with horrible body odor, and now the marrying off of every eligible lord and lady in the Lake District." She raised her moistening eyes to his. "There is no time in this world, Trevor. But there is a sense of never, a sense I'll never leave here."

If this woman was working with the people who stole the president, Trevor thought, she was performing superbly. They had obviously trained her well, but beyond her training she had some natural talent, a compelling quality that no amount of teaching could impart. Wary of her display of emotion, he kept up his guard against being seduced. It would be better, he thought, to play the part of the psychiatrist. Ask probing questions with feigned empathy to draw her out, and perhaps she'll inadvertently expose a clue that could help him find the president.

"Why do you think you're stuck here?" he asked.

Hannah shook her head and said slowly, "I'm a runaway character."

"What's that?"

"A cardinal no-no in genre fiction." She saw he didn't understand, so she elaborated. "Romance writers have to follow the rules of the genre. The woman gets her man. Or in your case, in the thriller genre, the hero gets the bad guy."

Trevor perked up at this. "The bad guy. Do you know who he is?"

"The president is the bad guy," Hannah said.

"No, the president is the guy I'm trying to find. Do you know who took him?"

"He took himself," Hannah said. "That's the big twist in chapter sixteen."

"That's impossible," Trevor scoffed. "The president can't kidnap himself."

"That's why it's such a good twist," Hannah said. "No one sees it coming."

"OK." Trevor shook his head once more as if trying to shake off the impossible logic of a dream, or the spell of a beguiling witch. She's doing it again, he told himself. She's telling you things you want to hear so she can mislead you. Turn the subject back to her. See what she'll reveal about herself.

"Why do think you're stuck here?" he asked again.

"I already told you."

"Why can't Wanda write you out of this?"

"Because she's depressed. She just lies around the house all day and smokes pot."

"How do you know that?"

"Go outside and smell the fog. It reeks of marijuana." Hannah paused for a moment, deep in thought, then added, "She's stuck. Poor Wanda is stuck."

"But you said she just finished the ninth book in the Regency series."

"It's horrible," Hannah said. "The first three were great, then they dried up. She's still sticking with the formula, but all the life has gone out of them. Only her diehard fans read her now."

Watching her there beneath the lamplight, detached as she was, unselfconscious and lost in thought, Trevor began to reappraise her, not as an agent or a spy, but as a woman. She has some depth to her, he thought, though God only knows what madness lurks down there. She's pretty enough to manipulate any man, and I can't figure out what cards she's holding. She's like a poker player who might have a royal flush or might just have a handful of nothing. Or maybe she's just jokers all the way down, the kind who draws you so far into their insanity that *you* begin to feel insane.

Will she try to play the seduction angle, he wondered. That's the most obvious option, given her delusions of romance. A gentle probe might shed some light on that question. Make a suggestion and watch her face. Watch her body. Don't listen to the words. Just look at the physical reaction.

"Maybe," Trevor offered in a gentle tone. "Maybe Wanda sent me here to be your lover. Your..." he fumbled through the words. "Your soulmate."

"No," Hannah said, shaking her head numbly. If there was any tell in her body language or facial expression, the weight of her sadness and resignation covered it up. He couldn't read her.

"You're in a different book," she said. "Remember? You don't belong here."

Here we go with the books again, Trevor thought. It's like we're running in circles. How do psychologists have the patience to deal with crazy people?

"And besides," Hannah added glumly, "you don't even have a penis."

Why did those words strike such terror into his heart? What power did she have over him that she could say something so patently ridiculous and yet make him feel compelled to check? To make sure?

The fog outside was thickening. The wisp that drifted in through the window sash smelled of marijuana, just as Hannah had said it would.

If she's right about that... Trevor thought nervously. He put his right hand on his thigh as nonchalantly as he could, and watched her to see if she noticed.

I don't care if she's in a book, he thought. And I don't care if I'm in a book, or if there is no time or if the whole world is just fog, but I'm not going to check my pecker just because some crazy woman whose dress changes color for no reason at all says I don't have one.

She watched his hand slide toward his crotch, and he watched her, pretending not to move it and seeing whether she was buying his ruse.

So what if one minute it's midnight and the next minute it's daylight, he thought. That doesn't mean I don't have a penis. People in Sweden have penises and it's light at twelve-ten a.m. on the summer solstice.

Hannah now seemed to have caught the contagion of his suspense. She watched his hand slide closer.

"I'm only doing this," said Trevor, who had broken into a sweat, "to prove that you're insane."

Hannah nodded kindly, wide-eyed with anticipation.

Finally, Trevor's hand hit the spot. He closed his eyes and let out a huge sigh of relief. "You're wrong!" he exclaimed with a delighted smile.

"Then you haven't gotten to chapter sixteen yet."

Trevor's eyes shot open. "What?"

"Chapter sixteen of *The President Has Been Stolen*."

"What's that supposed to mean?" Trevor said nervously. "What happens in chapter sixteen?"

"You'll find out."

2

Wanda Wiley sat on the edge of the bed beside a hamper of dirty laundry from which she had extracted four pairs of her almost-husband's underwear. She counted seven days back to the last wash.

He's getting better, she thought. Four pairs in seven days. When we first started dating, he'd only change them once or twice a week.

For six and a half years, her almost-husband had disappointed her by not proposing. In six months, they would have been together seven years, she thought, and their relationship would be a common-law marriage.

She wondered how many of her friends had started washing their partner's laundry three weeks into the relationship. Then she wondered if there was a socially acceptable way of asking that. It was a simple enough question with a straightforward answer. Why shouldn't she be able to ask it directly?

She pictured herself asking friends over drinks. How long into the relationship before you started washing his underwear? The scene played out like a movie in her mind.

She saw her friends read too much into the question, and she became embarrassed. Wanda shook off the daydream with some difficulty. The pot always made her imagination vivid.

As she smoothed a pair of red plaid boxers on the bedspread, the voice of her friend Louise returned from the recently dissolved scene and said, "I will never wash any man's underwear."

Fucking Louise, Wanda thought. She's so full of shit.

Wanda went to the door and turned off the overhead light. She opened the nightstand drawer and removed a little wand that her almost-husband had quietly assumed was a glow-in-the-dark vibrator. It was in fact an ultraviolet light used by campers and hunters to make stream water potable by killing all the bacteria in it.

Wanda passed the wand slowly over the red plaid boxers and counted four glowing stains. She picked up the pencil and tiny spiral notebook from the nightstand and read over her notes.

Sunday: Red plaid boxers. Sex - twice.

She put a check mark at the beginning of the line and tossed the boxers back into the hamper.

The black boxers came next. He had worn those on Monday. The ultraviolet light showed no stains. Her notebook said Dirk had gotten drunk on Monday night at a faculty event while Wanda got high and binge-watched *Orange is the New Black*. She didn't have to add "no sex." That was implied.

As she tossed the black boxers into the hamper, she wondered why the university served alcohol at Monday night faculty events, and what went on there that would encourage a man to get drunk.

Dirk was an erratic drinker. He'd go weeks without a taste of alcohol, and then for no reason at all, he'd get plowed.

"Why do you do that?" she asked. "What sets you off?"

"Nothing sets me off. When the Dirkster wants to get tanked, the Dirkster gets tanked."

"I hate it when you call yourself the Dirkster."

The next item to be examined was the pearl-white G-string, a garment that made her shudder. She called it his gay stripper underwear and asked him never to wear it in her presence. He said it was the most comfortable option in hot humid weather: "like a bra for my man parts" (his words) "to hold them up and keep them fresh."

The wand revealed several glowing stains on the G-string. Her notebook showed no entry that week for the stripper panties, and to her recollection, it had not been hot or humid. She checked the weather on her phone to be sure. The hottest day of the week had been Wednesday. Seventy-five degrees with twenty-nine percent humidity. Neither hot nor humid.

She wondered who he was keeping his man parts fresh for, and how fresh they needed to be. Was it the dark-haired Claudia with the coal-black eyes and extra-tight shirts? Or Jeanette, the sporty blonde? Or some other student she hadn't met yet? She was sure it was a student. They were easier to impress than women Dirk's own age, and Dirk needed to be admired.

Wanda pictured the blonde-haired Jeanette peeling the pearl-white G-string off Dirk's man parts, taking a long sniff and then smiling like a woman in a laundry detergent commercial. "Mmmm. How do you keep it smelling so fresh?"

She shook off the image with some difficulty and jotted a few words in the notebook. *G-string = cheat pants.* The image of the sniffing woman she had just dismissed came back and made her brow furrow. She jotted another note. *60/40 indica/sativa blend makes images TOO VIVID!! Do not want to see woman sniffing man parts.*

There was one pair of underwear left. The cobalt-blue briefs from last Friday showed unexplained stains. She tried to remember where Dirk had been that day.

Running errands, he had said. For six hours. But he didn't come home with any groceries or new clothes or anything else a person might pick up during six hours of errands.

After she threw the laundry in, she went into the office she had converted from the spare bedroom on the first floor. The room contained a small desk with a laptop and chair, a keyboard, monitor, lamp, a side table, and bookshelves.

The top shelf held the complete plays of Shakespeare. Thirty-seven cheap paperbacks, each marked up with highlights and underlines. They were the only books she read more than once. She also had a book of his longer poems, but she had lost the sonnets when she moved into the house and had never gotten around to buying a new copy.

The lower shelves held three or four copies of each of her eighteen titles, all mass-market paperbacks printed on pulp. She had written and published them in the six and a half years since she'd been with Dirk.

"I don't understand how you can crank them out so fast," he said at breakfast one recent morning through a mouthful of cold leftover steak.

"I put in six hours every day," Wanda said. "It's just a question of getting your ass in the chair."

Dirk glanced down at her ass when she said that. It was a subtle gesture that was meant to be noticed, characteristic of Dirk's manipulative tactics, reminding Wanda that her ass wasn't what it had been six and a half years ago, when she was a twenty-one-year-old student in Dirk's senior seminar and he had seduced her.

He was ten years older than her, and he was no stuffy professor. He dressed well and kept in shape. He had the broad shoulders and muscled chest of the shirtless models who would later grace the covers of her *Taken* series. And he seemed to always have a glow about him, as if health and vitality radiated from his perfect skin and golden hair.

And he's still like that, she thought. Because he works so damn hard at it. Ninety minutes of every day devoted exclusively to hygiene, and two hours to exercise. He looks just like he did when we met. But me...

The years of increasingly heavy pot smoking had made her lazy and chronically inactive. It had changed her diet from fresh greens to packaged cupcakes, cookies, ice cream, and chips. Her friends told her she was depressed, but the pot kept her mind entertained with visions that sometimes turned into books and mostly kept her amused throughout the day.

"Maybe I am depressed," she told her friends, "but I have a hundred and fifty channels in my brain that run twenty-four-seven. Sometimes all of them at once."

Dirk chewed through his mouthful of cold rubbery steak that morning and gave her a jab she should have seen coming. "It's not that you have your ass in your seat six hours a day. It's that you're writing to a formula. You don't have to put any thought into it. That's why you can whip them out one after the other, like pulling toilet paper off a roll."

"Why do you have to be such a jerk?"

Dirk shrugged and said with a disarming smile, "I don't know. Just born that way, I guess." One of the many maddening things about him was that when he insulted himself like this, it made her feel like he was bringing her into his confidence, and that made her smile. He had the charm of a snake, an arrogant self-confidence that would retreat at the most unexpected moments into self-deprecating humor, making people smile when they wanted to hate him.

Elements of his personality appeared in the scoundrel-heros of all the happily-ever-after pulp novels that lined the shelves of Wanda's office. She thought of him as a muse, a man as fascinating as he was infuriating. The sunshine of his love lit her world, while the icy indifference of his anger made her want to crawl into a hole and die.

The therapist she had seen in the third year of their relationship said, "From what you've described, it sounds like he has elements of borderline personality disorder. You know: I hate you, don't leave me. But he's too controlling to be borderline. He's a narcissist."

"I know," said Wanda.

"Why do you stay with him?"

"Ha! Have *you* ever slept with him?"

"But you don't want to be with him."

"Who says?"

"You. You're here."

"So?"

"So, why'd you come?"

She didn't like that question. It cut too close to the heart of the matter. She decided, with no basis in reality, that the therapist was in love with her and wanted to take her away from Dirk. So she stopped seeing him.

The therapist, with his textbook understanding of human relationships and his dry clinical vocabulary, could never understand the reality of being in love with a man like Dirk, who was at once infinitely needy and infinitely confident, a black hole that drained her emotional energy and then a supernova that could give it all back in one blinding burst.

"He's like a drug," she told Louise over coffee one morning.

"We can see that," Louise replied. "We can *all* see that. And what happens to drug users in the long run?"

Fucking Louise, with her fucking Volvo station wagon and her boring-ass milquetoast husband who sells insurance, and their twice-a-year flyaway vacations. Louise who eats oatmeal without sugar and drinks unflavored soy milk and gets socks for her birthday and LIKES it! Stupid bitch.

Yes, I crank out three books a year, and yes, it's easy because I love what I do. I have a vivid, relentless imagination. And yes, there's a formula. I admit that. So what?

So what, Dirk Jaworski, Distinguished Professor of Flawless Grammar and Pedantic Punctuation at Third Rate University? I've published eighteen books and you've published one—which nobody even read! Wanda sat angrily at her desk and rubbed her temples. Just admit that I'm good at this, will you?

"It's Byrd State," said the voice of Dirk that had lodged its corrective presence inside her brain. "Call it by its proper name."

Oh, get out of my head, Wanda thought. Do you have to nag me when you're not even here?

Eighteen books, but she'd never gotten a starred review from Kirkus or Publisher's Weekly. Eighteen books, and she brought in more money than him, though he pretended not to know this, and she didn't bring it up for fear of wounding the narcissist's pride.

The bookshelf in Dirk's office held fifty copies of his one and only published volume, *OMG, I'm Like, Totally Illiterate: How Instant Messaging is Destroying the English Language*. That work, which consisted of more footnotes than text, had earned him a professorship at Byrd State, and had then gone on to be cited in a handful of other academic monographs.

Funny, Wanda thought, how in academia becoming a footnote is a measure of success.

For the past few years Dirk had been working on the book he hoped would seal his bid for tenure, an encyclopedic eight-volume history of the Oxford comma. His writing process was different from hers. For Wanda, the character was the unit of composition. What kind of character did you start with in chapter one? What kind of adversity did the character face? And how did the character change by the end? The act of writing was simply tracing the arc of change from A to B over two or three hundred pages of richly detailed human interaction.

Dirk was more particular. The fundamental unit of writing for him was the letter, and he spent months agonizing over what the first letter of his masterpiece should be.

Should it be A? Absolutely not. That was too common and too obvious. The alphabet itself began with A.

T and E were also out, as they were the most common letters in the English language, and no work of Dirk Jaworski's would ever be common.

Z was too obvious. To begin a book with the last letter of the alphabet—that was just being contrary.

He had settled on X, in part because no book he knew of began with the letter X, and in part because it represented a monumental challenge. How do you follow up such a bold opening as X? If he pulled it off, he'd be famous.

But this was where things got difficult. What should the next letter be? If he chose E, he'd be stuck with an opening sentence about Xerox or Xenophon. The letter A would saddle him with Xanax or Xanthan gum. If he chose Y, he'd have to go with Xylophone, which smacked of childishness because every alphabet poster in every kindergarten classroom in the country showed a xylophone for the letter X.

Few people appreciated the enormity of the challenge he had set for himself in beginning his book with such a difficult letter.

He had been puzzling over the second letter of his masterpiece for four years now. Wanda brought snacks to his desk as he stared at the big black X on the top line of the otherwise blank page. She did all she could to encourage him.

"Maybe start with an outline," she suggested helpfully, but that just made him explode.

"Do you understand what it's like to have writer's block?"

"I'm just saying, back up for a minute and look at the big picture."

"You don't get it, do you? Because you can pump those books out like diarrhea. I'm trying to give birth here! Do you have any idea how fucking hard that is?"

"Don't shout at me, Dirk."

He slammed his hands down on the desk and made the keyboard jump. Then he grabbed his bag and stormed out of the house.

To the gym, Wanda thought.

He'd go pump iron for two or three hours and flirt with the girls in their leggings. Nothing made him happier than admiring his chiseled chest and shoulders in the weight-room mirror while he pumped and pumped and pumped himself up.

Then he'd come home and they'd have sex. She wondered if, during the act, he was thinking about her or one of the girls he saw in the gym. She knew he was most energetic on the days he was most frustrated with work. When his writing wasn't going well, she could channel his anger into sex. If she got him while his temper was good and hot, she could extract from him one of those nights that would turn stupid Louise Pennypacker green with envy and scare the hell out of her pudgy missionary-position husband.

All this was running through her mind as Wanda sat at her desk to begin the day's work. The monitor flickered on to a work in progress. She scrolled up though pages she didn't remember writing.

Why is Trevor in the house with Hannah, she wondered. Oh my god. This is way off script. This doesn't even make sense. She looked again at the outline of the book she was supposed to be ghostwriting.

In chapter eight of *The President Has Been Stolen*, the chapter she thought she had written yesterday, Trevor was supposed to be interviewing the president's mistress, Anna, at her house.

Anna.

Hannah.

God, how much pot did I smoke yesterday?

Wanda deleted the file and thought that was the end of it.

3

"OK, so let me get this straight. We're characters in a book, is that right?"

Hannah shook her head. "We're characters in the author's mind. Right now, we're parked, because the author doesn't know what to do with us."

"And this author is Wanda?"

"Yes. And I think she's starting to lose it. I think it's a combination of a bad relationship, too much pot, and too much isolation. Writers, you know, alone at their keyboards all day, living in their fantasy worlds."

"OK, but what happens in chapter sixteen?"

Hannah noticed Trevor's left hand was gripping his crotch tightly. She didn't remember it having moved since their conversation started, so he must have had it there the whole time.

"In chapter sixteen, you find the president."

Trevor grabbed her by the shoulders and shook her. "You know then! You know where he is!"

"I know where he is."

"Tell me!"

"Stop shaking me!"

"Sorry." He let her go. "Why can't you tell me?"

"It would ruin the suspense. Plus, you're only... Wait, where are you now?"

Trevor looked around at the elegant but aged furniture of the Victorian farmhouse, the thick fog licking at the windows. "In this godforsaken place."

"I mean, where in the book?"

"Come again?"

"What's the last thing you remember doing before you came here?"

Trevor turned and paced. "Let's see, um. Second floor of the East Wing. The president's wife tearfully confessed that he was having an affair—"

"With a woman named Anna."

"Yes," said Trevor, spinning on his heel to face her. "How did you know?"

"I told you, Wanda has the outline. I think that's how you wound up here. Wanda got high and her thoughts started skipping around. Anna to Hannah. You were supposed to go to Anna's house to interview her, but you came here instead."

Trevor looked up at the ceiling. Hannah could see he was thinking.

"If I could only remember how I got here," he muttered, "then I could get back."

Hannah shook her head.

"No? Why not?"

"Have you ever tried to retrace a train of thought you had when you were stoned? I mean a long, rambling, irrational train of thought? You can't do it."

"I wouldn't know. I don't use drugs. Where is the president?"

"You'll have to find him on your own."

Trevor strode quickly to her and grabbed her by the shoulders again. "Damnit, the future of the free world is at stake!"

"No, he's a bad president."

A look of murder crept into Trevor's eyes. "He's the best damn president we've ever had. And you're a traitor for letting him die!"

"I think you're being a little dramatic. Take your hands off me." She pulled herself away. Then she explained it to him.

"Look, Trevor, if I tell you where the president is, you'll go straight to him—"

"You're damn right I will!"

"—and that won't make any sense to the reader. The reader will flip back through the pages looking for clues that he missed, and he'll never find them."

"What reader?"

"The reader who's following you on your adventure."

Trevor went to the window and peered into the fog. "Who's following me? And how would you know about it?"

"God, you're dense! How do all those women fall for you?"

"What women?" Trevor asked absently.

"The flight attendants and the women in nightclubs, the foreign spies, the forensics experts. How do they all end up in bed with you?"

"I'm Trevor Dunwoody," he said. "The man who saves the world."

"Five times now," Hannah added. "And the only thing higher than your body count is your booty count. Let me tell you something, you've been living in a fantasy world."

"Excuse me? Haven't we both? You've been telling me this whole time we're in some author's imagination."

"You've been living in a world of *male* fantasy," Hannah said. "In the real world, not every woman is a hot babe. In the real world, the forensic scientist earns her position through brains and hard work. And not every woman falls into bed with a man just because he… he has a big pistol and is good at shooting it off."

"OK, that's enough lecturing," Trevor snapped. "This is the last time I'm going to ask. Where. Is. The. President?"

Hannah eyed him angrily. "You'll find him in chapter sixteen."

"Chapter sixteen?"

"Shh!" said Hannah. Then in a whisper. "Do you hear that?"

"Hear what?"

A soft, staccato tapping sound drifted faintly from above.

"There's someone upstairs," Trevor said.

"No," Hannah whispered. "That's the keyboard. She's writing."

"What's that supposed to mean?"

"Oh, this is not good. She shouldn't write when she's stoned. She really shouldn't."

"Tell me about chapter sixteen," Trevor said. The sound of the typing was getting louder.

"Not now. You're going to disappear in a few seconds."

"How do you know?"

"They all do. Everyone who comes here. They show up when she's stuck. They disappear again when she writes."

"Wait," said Trevor. "You have to tell me about chapter sixteen."

"I told you, I can't tell you where the president is. It'll ruin the story."

"No, the other thing." Trevor's hand went back to his crotch and held on tightly. "What you said before. Just tell me this. Do I have a penis at the beginning of chapter sixteen?"

"Yes," Hannah whispered.

"And at the end?"

Hannah shook her head gravely.

"Oh, God." Trevor's face was white as a ghost.

"Goodbye, Trevor."

He faded to nothing, but Hannah knew from the strong marijuana smell of the fog and the erratic tapping of the keys that Wanda's mind was not firing on all cylinders. Trevor would be back. A little wiser next time, she hoped.

4

At 6:18 p.m., Dirk flung himself through the front door and yelled "I'm home!" His voice had the unnecessary forcefulness of a four-year-old announcing itself to the mother whose life (he was sure) came to a screeching halt whenever he wasn't around. When Wanda first met him, she thought this was simply his dramatic way of entering the lecture hall, a way of grabbing the students' attention. But in the early days of their affair, she learned that he passed through every door as if an expectant audience awaited him on the other side. She suspected that in his mind he heard the crowd burst into applause at his appearance, the way theatergoers do when the star of the show first struts onto the stage. He even walked into the bathroom that way in the morning, as if the towels had spent the night in trembling expectation of his return.

He was supposed to have been home at 5:30. He hadn't called or texted to say he'd be late, so Wanda went ahead and made dinner—a special dinner that she was suddenly self-conscious about. What if he didn't like it? She felt the urge to explain her strange choice of food.

I was in the grocery store (all this went through her mind in a flash). And we always eat the same things. Chicken and fish and steak and pasta. And there were live lobsters in the tank, and that's something different, isn't it? They taste good with butter, and my mouth was so dry from the joint I'd just smoked... But I couldn't cook a live lobster. It seems so cruel. So I got two tails. They were frozen. The biggest ones in the store and...

She had broiled the lobster tails, timing them to be ready for Dirk's arrival at 5:30. She'd spent the past forty-eight minutes trying to keep them warm without having them dry out. She texted once to ask when he'd be back, but he didn't respond. She knew not to text again because that would be nagging. Better to languish in uncertainty than face one of his angry outbursts.

She had spent the empty time scrolling through Facebook, looking at the perfect beach photos of stupid Louise Pennypacker and her stupid boring husband who—surprise!—were going to have a baby! And oh my God, everyone, isn't it fucking wonderful? Isn't it 95 likes and 380 hearts and 66 gushing comments worth of WONDERFUL?

Just for the thrill of it, Wanda, stoned and angry, typed a nasty comment that she didn't intend to send.

Congratulations! Any idea who the father is?

Her finger had been hovering over the screen, ready to delete the message, when Dirk's sudden entrance startled her into tapping the Send button.

Oops.

"What's for dinner?" Dirk yelled as he banged around in the front hall.

"Can't you smell it?"

"Fish?"

Wanda stepped into the hall. "Lobster. What took you so long?"

"I didn't take long," Dirk said, brushing past her without a kiss or even a look. "Took me ten minutes to walk home, just like always. Did you do the laundry?"

"You said you'd be home at five thirty."

Dashing up the stairs, Dirk called, "What am I, a clock?" Judging from the sound of his footsteps on the bedroom floor, she calculated that he had stopped at the foot of the bed.

The laundry was still there, she thought. All folded, but—should she have put it away? Would he be annoyed? He paused there a moment, then his steps came quick and loud across the floor and down the stairs.

"If you wanted a *predictable* man"—his pronunciation of the word *predictable* was dripping with scorn—"you should have married Peter Pennypacker. What's for dinner?" He had already blown through the hall and into the kitchen.

"I just told you. Lobster."

She walked into the kitchen to see him plunging a fork into the larger of the two tails in the open oven. He tried to cram the tail into his mouth, but quickly yanked it out.

"Why's it so hot?"

"Are you in a hurry?"

"Obviously."

"Why?"

"I have to advise a student on his senior thesis. Four years into college and the kid doesn't know the difference between to, too, and two."

Dirk shook his head and continued, his mouth going smack-smack-smack as he worked through the piece he had just bitten off. "That's why the university has a grammar and punctuation department. Without me, books would look like texts. Three hundred pages"— smack,

smack, smack—"all one paragraph. No capitalization." Nom nom nom. "Poo emojis."

"Austin called."

"That loser?" Dirk bit off another chunk of meat, which he swallowed after only three chews. "What does he want?"

"He wants to talk to you, I guess. They're letting him go."

"No surprise," Dirk said, filling a glass of water at the kitchen sink. "He was adjunct. They hang on like convicts in a noose. They think getting fired is the end of the world, but it's a mercy killing. What's he going to do next?"

"I don't know. He's stopping by around nine."

Dirk chugged down the glass of water he had just filled, then said, "Won't be here."

"Where are you going?"

"I told you. I have to advise a student."

"But it's not even six thirty. He can't need three hours of advice."

"The kid's really confused." Dirk grunted. "And you know how I feel about homonyms."

He swept past her as she stood by the fridge with her arms folded across her chest. He flung open the pantry door and blurted, "Where's the bread?"

"It's right in front of you, Dirk. What am I supposed to tell Austin?"

"Tell him what I told him years ago." Dirk blew past her again and slapped the loaf on the counter beside the oven. "Biochemistry is a loser discipline. It's got nothing going for it. If he wanted a career in academia, he should have taken my idea."

For the first time since he'd come home, Dirk faced her directly. Wanda knew the look. It wasn't the one she wanted. Not the nice to see you, how was your day look.

He was checking to see if he had his audience's full attention because he was about to deliver a lecture.

"He has that useless scientific mind," Dirk said. "I told him, you want a long-term career, here's an idea: the politics of integers. No one's tackled that one yet. I mean, people don't even ask why one always comes first. They take it for granted. It's a totally unexamined assumption, and he could have blown it wide open. How do you think the number two feels, always having to play second fiddle? Talk about oppression! And don't even get me started on the marginalization of seven, eight, and nine. I mean, it's fucking arbitrary. Why can't people decide for themselves what order the numbers should go in? Do we have any mayonnaise?"

Wanda was so caught up in the fervor of his oration that she opened the fridge and handed him the mayonnaise without thinking.

Dirk laid two slices of bread on the counter and slathered them with mayo.

"I mean, I *gave* him that idea. Said he could take credit for it. Own it. Stamp his name all over it until his name was synonymous with the discipline, like Derrida and deconstruction. Instead he decides to study molecules."

Dirk turned and looked her in the eye to drive home his point. "Seriously! Molecules!" He shook his head in dismay. "Like they ever mattered on any level, anywhere in the universe. You gonna eat that other lobster tail?"

"I was planning on it."

"You don't want it," Dirk said. "It's dry. You cooked it too long."

Wanda felt her face flush and could hear the blood rushing through her ears. The slow-burning rage that had been building since she examined the laundry that morning was about to explode as she watched Dirk lay the second tail on the bread. He slapped the second slice of bread on top, then wrapped the sandwich in a paper towel.

Before she could speak, he had flown past her into the hallway with long, full strides.

"What am I supposed to eat?" Wanda yelled.

"Salad," Dirk called. "The fiber will help flush out the cupcakes you've been eating all day."

Wanda chased him through the hall and caught his sleeve before he could open the door.

"Where are you going?" she demanded.

"I told you."

"I don't believe you."

"Don't be shrill."

"I'm not being shrill!" she pleaded. In her attempt to suppress the shrillness of her tone, the words came out sounding pathetic.

Dirk's whole manner changed as he looked her in the eye. His air of hurry melted away. His posture relaxed, his shoulders went down, his face softened, and his eyes filled with warmth.

"Look, I know I've been busy lately. I know you've been alone a lot, and you've been struggling with your writing. I want to take you out tomorrow night. It'll do you good to be around other people. Get out of your own head for a while. I was thinking that new place on eighth. The French restaurant."

"It's expensive."

"Who better to share it with, then? I mean, who else in this world is really worth it?"

She melted in the warmth of his gaze. It was like a sun that shone for her alone. His kiss bestowed the enveloping warmth she had tried to recapture again and again in the joints she smoked after breakfast, lunch, and dinner.

She kept her eyes closed, wanting to hold on to him, but he slipped away, whispering playfully, "Off to enlighten the world." And then he was out the door. She watched him go down the walk. When he reached the sidewalk, she quietly opened the door and snuck out onto the porch. Her eyes would follow him until he turned the corner and disappeared.

But halfway to the corner, leaning against the hood of a neighbor's car, was a young brown-haired girl she had never seen before. She smiled as Dirk approached, uncrossed her arms, and pushed her slim hips away from the car. Wanda recognized the admiring upward tilt of the girl's face as he handed her the sandwich. She could see the beaming smile from half a block away, and though she couldn't see the expression in the girl's eyes, she knew it was the same starstruck look she herself had worn in the early days of his seduction.

At twenty-one, Wanda had been shy, inexperienced, and hopelessly romantic. Love, she imagined, would be the answer to everything, the magic power that would cure her shyness, unlocking her rich inner world to blossom into the light of day.

The magnificent professor, the wise and charismatic one, was the first person who had been perceptive enough to see inside her, to know her thoughts and feelings. She felt blessed, flattered beyond words, that this man of seemingly infinite confidence had chosen her, Wanda Wiley, above all other women.

She remembered the giddy excitement of entering the classroom of the man who projected such energy and vitality, of wondering what he would wear that day, whose paper he'd read aloud as an example of stellar or atrocious writing. There was no "good" or "bad" in Dirk Jaworski's classroom. Only superlatives. Grammatically correct sentences were "stupendous." Misplaced commas were "horrific."

She was volunteering in the theater that semester, making costumes for *Romeo and Juliet* as she daydreamed incessantly of the man who would soon take her to his bed. He had pulled her from her own uneventful existence into the drama of his life, where she would be by his side at the center of a whirlwind.

In the fervid imagination of inexperience, her opinion of him grew to be as grand as his opinion of himself. Watching the rehearsals, she found that Juliet's words described the intensity of her infatuation.

> Give me my Romeo; and, when he shall die,
> Take him and cut him out in little stars,
> And he will make the face of heaven so fine
> That all the world will be in love with night
> And pay no worship to the garish sun.

She copied the words into her journal and decided then she wanted to be a writer.

Now she wondered if this was what the new girl felt. That she had been chosen. That a new world was about to be opened up for her by this man.

Wanda knew the pattern. The new girl would hold Dirk's interest for a week or a month, and then he'd be onto the next conquest, in search of some new admirer to reinflate the ego that required constant affirmation.

As she watched them round the corner with a lightness in their step that made them appear to glide, the heaviness in her heart overwhelmed the bitter hatred that would have been the dominant emotion in a person less depressed.

She went upstairs and glanced at the neatly folded laundry on the bed, just to confirm what she already knew.

The pearl white G-string was missing. That's what he had gone upstairs to retrieve when she heard him stop at the foot of the bed.

Who's to blame for this, Wanda asked herself. You know who he is. You knew after the first year, when you stopped lying to yourself. Louise Pennypacker has been after you forever to leave him. Stupid Louise, who doesn't know a thing about passion, who doesn't understand that the only cure for my misery is the person who causes it. Stupid Louise and her stupid fucking baby. God, I hate myself. I fucking hate myself.

She rolled a fat, sticky joint and smoked herself unconscious.

Hannah, alone in her faded Victorian farmhouse, saw the world go dark in the thickening fog. For years, Hannah had thought that what she felt in these hours of darkness was fear, but today, somehow she understood that it was grief and despair.

Please let him learn something, Hannah whispered. Please let that fool Trevor Dunwoody gain some depth of character, some modicum of human understanding. Because my heart is breaking, and I need to tell someone.

5

Hannah awoke on the couch in her blue satin sweep-me-away dress. Someone was opening drawers in the kitchen. Trevor? Or some other wayward character who had fallen through the cracks of Wanda's imagination? Hannah listened quietly, careful not to make a sound. Silverware clanged as a drawer slid open and then banged shut.

That better not be one of those awful alpha males from the *Taken* series, Hannah thought. I'll stab him if he comes near me.

How long had she been asleep? She looked at the pearl and gold face of the stately grandfather clock, the clock that ticked eternally without ever being wound. Like all the clocks in the house, it had no hands. She looked to the window, but there was only the timeless pale fog that could indicate morning, midday, or afternoon.

Her heart sank. "I'll never get out of here," she muttered.

Trevor's voice came from the kitchen. "You awake?"

Hannah's dress rustled as she sat up. "I am now. Where were you?"

Trevor appeared in the doorway with a half-eaten peanut butter sandwich in hand. His jaw was working on the piece he'd just bitten off, which as far as Hannah could tell was about three proper mouthfuls. After forcing some of it down his throat, he said, "Where's the fridge in this house?"

"There isn't one."

"What the hell?"

"The house is a castoff, like me. It was the setting for a pre–World War I romance that Wanda abandoned. Where did you go? Back to your story?"

"Yeah."

Trevor stuffed the remaining half of the sandwich in his mouth and licked his fingers as he chewed with both cheeks bulging. Hannah noted how utterly unsuitable he was as a romantic lead, though she granted that his crude physicality was in some ways more realistic than the swaggering grace of Wanda's more idealized heroes. He was, after all, created by a man. *The President Has Been Stolen* was to be the sixth in Ed Parsippany's bestselling Trevor Dunwoody series. The other authors had done a good enough job of bringing the first five outlines to life. Wanda was the first woman to have a crack at the franchise.

"Where'd you leave off?" Hannah asked.

Trevor said something incomprehensible through a wad of sandwich that would have choked a dog.

"Finish chewing before you talk," Hannah said.

Impatient to get his words out, Trevor swallowed the whole mouthful at once. His eyes went wide as the giant bulge stuck in his throat, and Hannah's eyes went wide watching him. Quick as a flash, her mind ran through two alternate scenarios:

He chokes, and I leap up and save him. Heimlich maneuver, followed of course by mouth-to-mouth. But no… If Wanda's had any hand in forming him, he'll fall in love with me for saving him, and then I'll be stuck here forever trying to fend him off. Ew! She winced at the thought of it.

Other option, he chokes, and I just sit here and watch him die. But then what happens to the body? There's no place to bury him. I can't throw him in the well, because I have to drink from there. Does he just rot in the living room? It's bad enough I have to languish in this place, but I can't stand strong odors. That would push me over the edge. Jesus, Trevor, swallow that fucking sandwich and don't die on me!

Trevor saw her let out a breath of relief as he got the food down. He wiped his mouth with the back of his hand, then wiped both hands on his pants. "Had you in suspense there, huh?" He smiled. "That's my specialty."

"What happened in the book?"

"Oh. Well, I talked to the president's mistress, Anna."

"And you screwed her."

Trevor cocked his head and gave her a funny look. "How'd you know that?"

"Because you screw every woman in your thrillers."

"No," said Trevor proudly. "Just the attractive ones. Wait, did you see? You weren't watching me do her in the bathroom, were you?"

"No, Trevor. I only know the outline of the story. And even if I could have watched, I wouldn't want to."

"Afraid you'd get turned on?"

"Not in the least. What happened after Anna?"

"I flew to Paris, following a lead, got shot at, then went to Moscow undercover."

Hannah thought through the outline to figure out how far into the story he was. "Is that where you left off?"

"No. I went back to DC. Had a meeting in the White House with the top brass. No sign of the president and no promising leads. We're at a loss. Right now, we have a stand-in, a look-alike going through the president's motions so the cameras can catch a glimpse of him now and then. We're keeping his disappearance under wraps so the public doesn't panic."

Hannah nodded. "So you're walking out of the White House. It's eleven thirty on a cool fall evening, and a mist is falling, leaving orange halos around the domes of the sodium lamps on Pennsylvania Avenue."

Trever looked surprised. "How the hell did you know that?"

"That part of the outline was very specific. Do you know what happens next?"

"What?"

"Chapter sixteen."

Hannah watched the anxiety rise in his eyes. His left hand slid to his crotch and clamped tightly around the package he was desperate to protect.

He began to ask a question, but broke off because his throat was dry. He swallowed hard and tried again. "What... Um... What happens to my wee-wee? Can you at least tell me? So I have a chance to protect myself?"

"I can tell you," Hannah said, "but you won't be able to protect yourself. If it's written, it's your destiny. It will happen and there's nothing you can do."

Trevor's face took on the look of dauntless determination that had kept his avid readers coming back for five straight books. "I'm Trevor Dunwoody, goddamnit, and when I want something to happen, I make it happen. Now tell me who's going to try to unman me and how, and I'll kill the bastard."

The moistness in his eyes belied the bravado of his words.

"Are you crying, Trevor?"

He nodded. "A little bit, yes."

"But you've always been so brave. You've saved senators, generals, the daughter of a foreign president. You saved the entire city of New York."

"But this is my winkie," Trevor pleaded. "Me and Willy have been together our whole lives."

Hannah smiled as she watched him squirm. "I do just fine without a willy."

"That's because you've never experienced the joy of having one. If you ask a blind man whether he misses the light, he'll say no, because he doesn't know what it's like."

Hannah got up from the couch and walked to where he stood in the doorway.

"Tell me, Trevor, how many women have you stuck that thing in?"

"I don't know. Fifty? Sixty?"

"Do you ever wonder what they see in you?"

"I'm Trevor fucking Dunwoody," he said proudly. "Every woman wants a piece of me."

Hannah circled to his left, watching him as an investigator watches a suspect under questioning. "Have you ever noticed there's not an ounce of courtship in your novels?"

"Who has time for courtship when you're saving the world?"

"Have you ever noticed there's not even a getting-to-know-you phase in any of your relationships? Or that every secretary, every concierge, every female cop and spy you have to deal with is young and beautiful? Have you ever noticed that after you bang them, and you bang every last one of them, you don't have to interact with them again?"

Trevor shrugged. "I didn't make the world I live in."

"No," said Hannah. "A man did. A man made your world, and in that world, every woman is just a hole waiting to be filled."

"I'm not complaining," Trevor said.

"Well I would never want to live in your world."

"Maybe that's why you're stuck here."

"Does it strike you as odd, Trevor, that your creator would take away your most prized possession? Little Willy there?" She clapped her hand on top of the hand that guarded his crotch.

"It's Willy," Trevor said. "Not *little* Willy. And yes, it makes no sense. What kind of hero has no pecker?"

"Wonder Woman," Hannah said. "Clarice Starling. Princess Leia. Sigourney Weaver."

"Yeah, but those are chicks. I'm Trevor fucking Dunwoody!"

"You want to know what happens, Trevor? I'll tell you what happens. You're going to find the president in the next chapter. You'll stumble on him unexpectedly, and when you try to take him back, he's not going to want to go. The president stole himself, remember? That's the twist. You try to take him back and he shoots your penis off."

Those words sent a jolt of terror down Trevor's spine. He tried hard not to show his anguish. "The president," he said through clenched teeth, "is an old military friend. He was my CO in the Marines. He would never shoot my pecker off."

"Would you like to bet on that?"

"And besides, my author... What's his name?"

"Ed Parsippany."

"He would never do that to me."

"But he's not writing this one."

"But he wrote the outline. And your, what's her name, Wanda, has to write to the outline."

Hannah turned her back to him as she walked toward the couch. "That's just it," she said, then turned again to face him. "She won't stick to the outline. She's distraught and stoned and no longer in control of what she writes."

"How do you know?"

"Because I know her, Trevor. I live in the subconscious that she keeps ignoring. She hates domineering men. She used to be attracted to their confidence and certainty, to their vigor, but now she detests them. And the next time you step into your story, she's going to blow your cock right off."

Trevor said nothing, but she could see he was trembling. For a moment, she pitied him.

"If it's any consolation," she offered, "I like being a woman."

Trevor began to sob.

6

Wanda awoke to the sound of the doorbell, rising slowly from her sprawl atop the folded laundry on the bed. The remains of the joint had burned a hole through one of Dirk's shirts.

"Jesus," she muttered. "Lucky I didn't burn the house down."

She looked at the clock as the bell rang again. 9:03 p.m. That would be Austin ringing, coming to talk to Dirk.

Wanda stood and wavered for a moment. The pot had lowered her blood sugar and she craved sweets. She pushed her hair from her face and didn't bother looking in the mirror. She knew she looked like shit in her baggy sweats and oversized t-shirt, with her ratty hair and bloodshot eyes.

Should she put on a bra? The bell rang again.

No. It's just Austin. I'll tell him Dirk's not here. Tell him to go away.

She wasted no time when she opened the door.

"Dirk's not here."

"I know."

"Then... Wait, why are you here?"

"You want to walk over to the store with me?"

"No. How did you know Dirk's not here?"

"Because I just saw him drinking wine at a café with one of his students."

"No, you didn't."

"OK." Austin shrugged. "I didn't. You want to walk with me to the store?"

"What's her name?"

"Shana. When's the last time you were out?"

"Why?" She touched her face. "Do I look pasty?" She glanced at him to gauge his response and considered shutting the door in his face. "I was out a few hours ago," she said defensively. "What do you care?"

"Where'd you go?"

"Here. The porch. I watched Dirk go to his meeting."

"With Shana?"

"Is that her name?"

Austin leaned in to get a closer look at her eyes in the semi-dark. "You're stoned."

"A little."

"Walk with me to the store."

Wanda hesitated.

"I know you have a sweet tooth," Austin said. "I'll buy you a lemonade."

In the three blocks between the house and the neighborhood store, they hardly talked. The sounds of the crickets and the insects in the trees struck Wanda as unusually vivid, and she remembered that she used to hear those sounds every night in the spring, back in the years when she used to get out in the evenings.

She glanced at Austin and wondered how often he heard these noises, how often he was out at night, and whether his life had some dimension hers lacked.

He's plain, she noted, as she looked at the stubble on his face. Plain and average in every way except for intellect. Average height, average build, average looks, with an undistinguished voice you couldn't pick out of a crowd. Dresses like the J. Crew catalog from four years ago. Dwells in his work, like me.

He didn't mind her looking at him any more than she minded him looking at her.

"I heard you lost your job."

"No," said Austin, opening the door to the mini-mart. The glaring fluorescent lights made her wince. "I gained a job."

"Oh?"

"You want a soda?"

She shook her head. "Lemonade. You put the idea in my head and I can't stop thinking about it."

They walked to the drink cooler. "I'm glad you found something," she said. "I was worried you were dropping by for sympathy. I don't have any to give these days."

"I know." He pulled two bottles of lemonade from the cooler and handed her one. She opened it immediately and took a sip. She wanted to follow up on that *I know*. You know what, she wondered as they made their way to the register. That I'm the girlfriend of a narcissistic prick?

"Dirk is a narcissistic prick," Austin said.

"God, I hate when you do that!"

"Do what?"

"Read my mind. Stay out of there."

"It's public knowledge," Austin said as he laid a five on the counter.

"So?" Wanda shrugged.

Outside the store, she felt the tension leave her body, the tension of being stoned beneath the too-bright lights that exaggerated the popping colors of the junk food packages. The dark air was warm and moist. The song of the crickets wove itself into the fabric of the night.

I've been shut up in that office too long, she thought. Shut up in the stale air of that stale room. In the stale thoughts of my stale mind. Please don't ask me how my writing is going. I know you're going to ask, Austin, because there's nothing else to talk about with me, but please don't ask.

"How's your writing going?"

"Like shit. Can we turn left here?"

"Take the long way home?"

"It's a nice night."

They walked in silence for half a block, and to her surprise she blurted, "It's incoherent." She stopped and thought about backing up, thought about giving him some context, since his own thoughts had probably been wandering and he might not know that she was still talking about her writing, that her writing was incoherent.

But he knew.

"Doesn't surprise me," he said.

"What do you mean?"

"You're a mess."

"And you're unemployed."

"No," he said. "I got a job. Remember? I told you that."

"Where?"

"On the porch, when we were talking at the door." He gave her a concerned look, a look that asked how much pot she'd been smoking lately.

"No, where's the job?" she asked.

"California."

She stopped. "Really?"

"Yeah."

"What, um..." Her voice caught and the words stuck in her throat. She had never considered the idea of him leaving. "A university?" She drank most of the rest of the lemonade and wished she had another.

Austin shook his head. "A private company. A startup that uses new technology to examine biochemical processes."

"That's exciting."

As they started walking again, he asked tentatively, "What was... what was that in your tone just now?"

"I didn't have a tone," she said coldly. "When are you leaving?"

"In a few days."

She stopped again and tried to think of something to say to cover up her sense of loss. She didn't want to encourage that long simmering feeling that he was always hiding from her. Always so incompetently hiding.

"I always dreamed of living there someday," she said. "By the sea, without the bitter winters and the oppressive, steaming summers."

She rebuked herself inwardly. Jesus, you fool, why don't you just beg him to invite you?

Fortunately, he didn't read her remark as she had feared, or if he did, he wasn't going to follow up on it.

"And you're staying here?"

"I'm staying right here," she said. She drained off her last ounce of lemonade as they rounded a corner. In one more block, she'd be at her door, telling him goodnight. And in a few days, he'd be gone.

They walked in silence that final block, and she inwardly derided him for not having the nerve of Dirk Jaworski, for not just going after what he so obviously wanted—even though she knew he'd never get it. Half of her wanted him to try, dared him to try.

They made it all the way to the door without a word. She opened it, then turned and reached for his empty bottle. "Want me to take that?"

He handed it to her silently, and in the darkness, she couldn't make out the expression on his face.

"Can I tell you something?" he asked.

Just like Austin Reed to ask if he could tell me something, she thought. If you want to tell me something, then tell me. You're not like Dirk at all. Imagine Dirk asking: Can I put this in you? Don't ask permission. Show some confidence. Be a man.

She tried to puzzle out his intentions there in the dark, but all she could see was the silhouette of the man standing with both feet firmly planted on the ground. He was too far away to attempt a kiss. But then, he might just be the type to fumble into it from an awkward distance and wind up with his mouth against her nose.

"What is it?" she asked, tensing slightly in anticipation of him making a fool of himself.

"Do you remember the first time we talked?"

"Yeah."

"I called for Dirk. To tell him I got the job, that I'd be moving here. You answered and said he wasn't home, and then we talked for an hour."

"Get to the point."

"When I pictured coming here, the whole town, the university and everything, was colored with you."

"And what did you think?" she asked with a hint of scorn. "That you would come and seduce me away from Dirk?"

"I thought you were the loveliest human being I had ever encountered."

The words caught her off guard, landing like a blow, and stirred an instant rage that she struggled to contain.

"And what do you think now, Austin? After knowing me for two years? After watching the shit show of my life? How's your little fantasy doing now?"

Her words didn't shake him. He said simply, "If I never see you again, I want you to know that there's one person on this earth who thinks the world of you."

She turned and went inside without a word, closing the door on him.

She threw the empty bottles violently into the recycling bin in the kitchen, then pulled them back out with equal violence and threw them into the trash.

She ran upstairs and shut herself in the bedroom. She brushed the laundry from the bed in one angry sweep, then sat down, then got up and paced across the clothes she had spent the morning folding.

What a pathetic attempt at seduction, she fumed. *I think the world of you,* she mocked. Who cares what you think? You're bland and boring. You're Peter Pennypacker looking for his Louise. You're bald and... wait, you're not bald. Or pudgy. But you will be in a few years. Probably.

In her mind's eye, she saw herself in a polka-dot dress with Louise Pennypacker's idiotic 1950s housewife hairdo, and the rage in her heart swelled to a point that frightened her. She felt that if Austin Reed were to set foot in her room at that moment, she would kill him. She would kill Dirk too. She might even kill herself.

She looked at her hands.

Oh, God, I'm shaking.

I'm shaking.

She opened the top drawer of the nightstand and pulled out the bag of sticky green buds. She found the rolling papers, but her hands shook too much to roll a joint. She remembered the remains of the joint she had smoked earlier. The roach still had three good hits in it, but where was it? She tore through the laundry on the floor and found it, the paper soaked with brown resin.

Where was the lighter? There was one in the bathroom. She rushed in and picked it up from the counter by the sink. She sparked the flame and caught a glimpse of herself in the mirror, the roach stuck to her lip, her hands shaking, her face drawn and pale, eyes filled with rage and ringed with dark circles of depression and fatigue.

How could a little pass like that have set you off so badly, she wondered. So what if he hit on you? A hundred guys have hit on you. You shake it off. Who cares?

She let the flame go out. She took the roach from her lips and left it by the sink beside the lighter.

On the edge of the bed, she sat quietly with her eyes closed and ran though the encounter on the porch. What set you off, Wanda Wiley?

He didn't try to touch you. He wasn't rude or presumptuous. He simply said what he felt. And that was bold, wasn't it? It was bold of him to lay it on the line like that. Not like Dirk, with his false courage. Dirk who doesn't really put his feelings on the line, who spends days or weeks grooming his targets and then pounces only when he's sure he's already won. Dirk isn't a risk taker. He's a manipulator. He only goes after the types he knows he can get.

She felt bad about turning her back on Austin, shutting the door in his face. She realized in hindsight what had triggered her astonishing rage. In offering her an alternative to Dirk, Austin was trying to take something from her. He was taking the dream into which she had poured most of her energies these past six and a half years. The dream of making it work with Dirk, of capturing the heart he was incapable of giving, of winning the illusory prize that could never be won. Dirk's heart belonged to

Dirk alone. No one could seduce his love away from himself.

Dirk could get to her in many ways. Through fear, through her insecurities, through desire. He could turn her on against her will, even when she hated him. But he could not say, "I like your book." Or even, "I read your book." He could never have said, "I think the world of you," and even if he tried, he couldn't have meant it, because the only thing that mattered in Dirk's world was Dirk.

She couldn't shake the fear that Austin's words had put in her, the fear that she would have to abandon the central project of her life. That was the sore spot—realizing how much Dirk really had been the center of her life, that she had poured into him even more energy than she had poured into her writing. To walk away from Dirk would be to admit that all her energy had been wasted, that all her hopes had been illusory and vain.

How insolent of Austin to ask, to even suggest, that she do all that for him! She couldn't shake her anger at him, her resentment at the threat he posed to her hopes and dreams.

But his words had hit their mark, and there was no undoing the effect of knowing that someone truly cared.

7

Hannah slouched on the couch of the old Victorian farmhouse, contemplating the hygiene of wearing that blue satin sweep-me-away dress for what felt like four consecutive days. She could hear Trevor in the bathroom blubbering and talking to his man parts. "These could be our last hours together," he sniffed.

I wonder how long he can keep that up, she thought. He's been at it for thirty minutes. His morose complaints were beginning to bring her down. She tried to think of something to distract him.

The light coming through the crack in the curtains showed that the fog had thinned. Maybe a walk, she thought as she stood and approached the window, a walk in the timeless, spaceless fog will take his mind off his willy. I can't believe how much time he spends thinking about that thing.

She opened the curtains to a surprising scene. The fog had not only thinned, it had receded a good sixty feet from the side of the house to reveal rosebushes, not yet in bloom, and what looked like flower beds carved in curving lines between sections of thick green lawn. The beds were empty, but the dark soil was rich and promising. This was the most she'd ever seen of the house's surroundings.

She left the living room to knock on the bathroom door. She would encourage Trevor to go outside with her and have a look at the scenery. But first she paused to listen to the prayer he uttered with such anguished sincerity.

"Oh, Lord, you know I don't believe in you because anyone who would create so many tree-hugging hippies and self-righteous liberals has got a screw loose. But whatever. It's your universe. All I'm asking for right now is a little bargain. You let me keep my willy, and I'll turn my life over to you. I'll do whatever you want, except vote Democrat. I'll spread your word far and wide. I'll even read the bible. The whole thing. I'm *that* serious."

Hannah knocked. "Trevor?"

"Is that you, God?"

"No. Are you still crying?"

"Trevor Dunwoody doesn't cry!"

"Come out here."

"I'm busy."

"You sound sad. Come outside. I want to show you something."

"Oh, alright," he sighed.

She heard him zip his pants and then the door opened.

"Trevor," she said excitedly, "look at this."

She led him through the kitchen.

"How long until I go back into my book?" he asked. She was glad to hear some firmness returning to his voice, though she could still hear the fear.

"I don't know," Hannah said. "Whenever Wanda starts writing again." She opened the back door and they went out.

"Look!" she whispered.

The fog had receded to expose half an acre of lush green lawn, rhododendrons, and a towering magnolia. They both had to squint in the brightness of the day.

Hannah looked at him with wonder and whispered, "Something happened."

"Yeah," said Trevor. "That dweebus made a pass at her." His eyes fixed on the iron handle of the well pump, and an idea struck him in a blinding flash. "Salvation!" he cried. "Where are the tools?"

"What tools? And what dweebus? What are you talking about?"

"I'm talking about tools, baby!" His energy had flipped so quickly from morose to manic, she wondered if he was bipolar.

"There are some tools in the basement, but—"

Trevor dashed into the house before she could finish. She followed him in and from the kitchen could hear his footsteps thundering down the stairs.

She stopped at the top of the steps and called, "Trevor?"

"Profit!" he cried excitedly, and in a few seconds, he was on his way back up with a heavy wooden toolbox.

Hannah had to step out of the way to avoid being knocked over as Trevor sped toward the rear of the house with the tools.

Hannah went back through the kitchen and found him outside at the well. She pulled up her dress to keep the satin from catching on the splinters of the threshold as she exited.

"Trevor, what are you doing?"

"Man's work, honey. Step aside." He held an adjustable wrench to one of the bolts that attached the handle to the pump. The handle was about three feet long. At one end, it was fitted to the human hand. At the other end, the end

Trevor was working to detach, it flattened out to a triangular iron plate about six inches wide at the base and almost one inch thick.

"Who is dweebus?" Hannah asked.

Trevor grimaced as he forced the wrench down with all his strength.

"Joe Boring," Trevor said. He fell forward as the nut loosened, then he immediately attacked the second nut.

"What do you mean he made a pass at her? How would you know if someone made a pass at Wanda?"

"Didn't you hear them?"

"No," said Hannah, surprised.

Trevor lurched as the second nut loosened.

"You can hear their words?"

Trevor pointed up toward the sky. "Comes from the same place as the typing. You really didn't hear?"

"No! I've never known what she says aloud or what anyone says to her. I only get the feelings. And something happened. Something changed. I don't think she's fully aware of it because this is the sort of thing I always know first."

While she spoke, Trevor had loosened the nuts enough to start twisting them off with his fingers.

"Step back," he said. "This thing is heavy. I don't want it to fall on your feet."

"What are you doing with that? I need it to pump water."

"I'll bring it back." He slid the long iron handle from the bolts and his arms sagged under the weight of it.

"What did Joe Boring say?"

"I don't know. Some hapless pickup line. Total loser. Guy's got no game at all."

Trevor set the flat triangular base of the iron handle on the ground and opened the top button of his pants. For a moment, Hannah feared he might ask her to kiss Little Willy goodbye. But his attention wasn't on her. He lifted the heavy handle from the ground and slid the triangular base into the front of his pants. The handle stuck out of the top, almost up to his collar bone.

"I need a truss to hold this thing in place." Trevor patted the steel plate that protected his precious willy and said, "That's three quarters of an inch of iron. No one's going to shoot through that unless they have an assault rifle or a .44 Magnum. Hey, you don't know what kind of piece the president packs, do you?"

"I know nothing about guns. Trevor, who was Wanda talking to? And what did he say? This is important."

"I don't know. It was some guy, uh… Houston. Or Dallas. Or…"

The sound of clacking keys drifted down from above.

"Oh, shit!" Trevor exclaimed. "She's at the keyboard again. I need a truss or this thing's gonna slide down my pants leg. Do you have an industrial strength bra I could borrow?"

"There's no time. Trevor, what did Dallas say to her?"

"He said, um…" Trevor put on a mocking voice. *"You're the loveliest human being I've ever encountered, Wanda. I think the world of you.* Ha! In Trevor Dunwoody's world a line like that would put a guy in the friend-zone forever."

The clacking of the keys grew louder. Hannah grabbed him angrily by the collar and said, "Screw Trevor Dunwoody and his stupid game. He meant what he said, and she knew he meant it. That's why it got to her. That's why the fog has thinned and the day is bright. That's why the soil is rich and the bushes are green."

"Step away from the man," Trevor said, brushing her hands off. "I have a president to save."

Hannah grabbed him again. "Listen, buddy, I heard you praying in the bathroom just now, and I'll give you a little piece of advice. The god of this world is Wanda Wiley, and if you want something, you'll have to ask her. Your big iron dong shield will do you no good. She's furious with Dirk, more angry than she even knows, because she won't let herself feel what's really going on inside her. That's why I'm trapped here. And that's why she's going to blow your cock off. You're as domineering as he is.

"If you want to save your willy, you say a prayer to Wanda. You tell her that from now on Little Willy will be the last part of you that ever meets a woman. The first part will be your ears, and then your mind, and then your heart. You tell Wanda that, you make it a solemn vow, or Little Willy is history."

"Willy," Trevor corrected. "Not *little* willy."

And then he disappeared.

8

On a wet October evening, Trevor Dunwoody emerged from the black iron gate that separated the White House grounds from the brick and stone of Pennsylvania Avenue. The meeting in the East Wing had ended on a disquieting note. The CIA now believed that the Russians were not involved in the theft of the president. The leads in Paris had evaporated, and the FBI had cleared all of the white nationalist groups that had earlier been flagged as potential suspects. The president was simply gone.

Trevor trudged heavily through the thickening mist with both hands on his crotch to support the immense weight of the iron pump handle that protected his manhood. His thoughts drifted from his mission of finding the president to a more immediate concern. How long could he afford to tie up both hands supporting his fifty-pound willy shield? What if he needed to shoot someone, or shake the hand of a foreign dignitary?

"Psst!"

The hissing call came from the base of the statue of the Marquis de Lafayette just ahead. Trevor ignored it and trudged on.

"Psst!" The figure was eight feet in front of him now, wrapped in a dark tattered overcoat stuffed with newspaper to keep out the damp of the autumn night. The man's bearded face was smeared with filth, and he smelled of malt liquor.

"Fuck off," Trevor said. "I haven't got any money."

As he passed, the slouching lump of humanity whispered, "Trevor!"

Trevor stopped abruptly and turned in astonishment.

"Gary?"

"Yeah."

"Mr. President? What are you doing here?"

"I hate my fucking job." From the tatters of his overcoat, the president withdrew a giant .50 caliber Desert Eagle pistol and pointed it at Trevor's crotch.

"Where the hell did you get that?" Trevor asked, breaking into a cold sweat.

"I don't know. What's that sticking out of your pants?"

"Nothing!" Trevor blurted defensively.

"It looks like a giant phallus."

"Please don't shoot it."

The president racked the giant pistol, whose massive slugs could easily penetrate three-quarters of an inch of iron. Trevor began to shake uncontrollably.

"Why do you want to shoot me?" he asked.

"Because you screw every woman you meet."

"So do you."

"I know," said the president. "Makes no sense, does it? What was the name of the last woman you had sex with?"

"Um..."

"Think, Trevor, think!" The president whistled the theme to *Jeopardy* as Trevor stood trembling.

"I um..." Trevor felt his arms weakening. "I can't..."

"You can't remember?"

"Maybe if you pointed that gun away from me," he said. "It's kind of a high-pressure situation with the gun and the *Jeopardy* theme."

"But you're Trevor Dunwoody. The man who thrives on pressure. The man who never caves."

"But I love my winkie!" Trevor blurted.

"Who doesn't love their winkie?" asked the president. "But you have to use it responsibly. You have to earn the privilege to keep it."

Trevor's arms gave out, and the heavy handle slid down the left leg of his trousers, banging his kneecap before getting jammed in the narrow lower section of the pants.

"Trevor?"

"Yes, Mr. President."

"Are you crying?"

Trevor nodded.

"I'm really sorry to do this to you," said the president. "I mean, don't think I don't sympathize. But... I don't know. I feel like the world's gone crazy lately. Like the laws of the universe have changed. Like God walked away and left everything in the charge of some new spirit who might be slightly unhinged. You ever feel that way?"

At the mention of God, Trevor remembered Hannah's words. He dropped awkwardly to his knees, the pump handle hindering his movement. Then he turned his tearful eyes to heaven and said, "Lord, if you let me out of this one, I swear to you that from now on Little Willy will be the last part of me that ever meets a woman. The first part will be my ears, and then my mind, and then my heart. I solemnly vow."

He heard a click and saw the president slide the firearm back into his coat.

"That was a lovely prayer, Trevor."

"Thank you."

"You can take that thing out of your pants now."

Those were the magic words he once was able to draw from the lips of every woman he met. Now they had an entirely different meaning. He unzipped his pants, withdrew the large handle, and laid it on the bricks near the base of the statue.

Zipping his pants, he said, "Come on, Mr. President. You need to go back to the White House."

Gary shook his head. "No way, man. That's the worst job ever. You have no idea."

"Who stole you?" Trevor asked.

"No one. I made it look like a burglary. You know, open window, dresser drawers dumped out, wallet and cell phone missing, a couple expensive watches gone from the closet. Oh, and me. Classic in-and-out theft. Swipe the good stuff and scram."

"How did you get out?"

"That's *my* secret and I'm not telling. Want some malt liquor? I have a forty of Olde English 800 under my coat."

"I could use a drink," Trevor said. "My nerves are shot."

The president handed him the bottle. Trevor took a swig and spat it out at once. "That tastes like piss," he said, wiping his mouth.

"Sorry, wrong bottle. Try this one."

The second bottle contained malt liquor. Trevor drained off twelve ounces.

"Have you been hiding here the whole time?" Trevor asked.

"Not hiding," said the president. "Sitting in plain view."

"And no one's noticed?"

"The homeless are invisible. At least, under my administration. You know, it's funny seeing the world from this perspective. Everyone rushing around all stressed out, like their lives are so important. So important they don't take time to live. You ever watch the sparrows hop around and pick at crumbs on the sidewalk?"

"That would bore the shit out of me."

"That's what I used to think. But an hour of that is bliss compared to an hour of national security briefings. Absolute bliss. I'm beginning to understand why the Buddha sat still to find enlightenment. I used to think it was something you had to go out and grab by the balls."

"What'll happen if you don't go back?" Trevor asked.

The president shrugged. "Everything will proceed as usual. They'll put someone new in the role. Politics is like genre fiction, the same old story over and over. The characters and the setting change, but the plot is the same." He pointed up toward the clouds. "You hear that soft rhythmic tapping? That's God typing out our fate."

"You can hear that?"

"I never could until I had the time to sit here quietly and listen. Now I hear it on and off. It always kicks up when the world gets busy. That's when he's up there banging out the action."

"She," Trevor said.

"Huh?"

"She. It's a woman."

"Really?"

"It didn't used to be," Trevor said. "It used to be a man's world. The first five books, you could feel the testosterone coursing through every page. Now it's a woman spinning the yarn."

"So that's what changed. That's why the world feels so different."

"Well, now we have a problem."

"What's that?"

"If you don't want to go back to the White House, then what's my mission? Where does the book go from here? What's the plot?"

The president shrugged. "Does it matter?"

"It does to me. What good is Trevor Dunwoody if he has no one to beat up, no one to shoot, no one to screw?"

"You got me," said the president.

9

"What the hell is this?"

Wanda didn't recognize the voice of the angry, impatient woman coming through the phone. She wasn't entirely sure what time it was. The call had startled her awake there at her desk.

"I mean, seriously, what the fuck?"

The monitor had gone black when the computer went to sleep, probably around the same time she did. The dark crumbs on the white dinner plate were a bad sign. She had eaten an entire cake. And now she was hungry again.

"Who is this?" Wanda asked groggily.

The woman gave a name she didn't recognize, then after an impatient pause, she added, "Ed Parsippany's editor. What the hell are you doing with Trevor Dunwoody?"

"What?"

"You don't go shooting off the dick of our imprint's most profitable character."

"Oh God," Wanda said. "Did I pull the trigger? I can't remember."

"No, you didn't pull the trigger, thank God, but you need to rewrite that entire chapter. I mean, why the hell does Trevor have an iron handle sticking out of his pants? Where did that come from? He just walked out of a White House meeting with that thing? Are you stoned?"

"Well, yeah. Wait, I wrote that chapter just before I passed—before I took a nap. How did you read it?"

"You back everything up to Dropbox, remember? And I see everything in the Trevor Dunwoody folder. You know it's an honor to ghostwrite for Ed Parsippany. It's the kind of work that can launch a career."

"I already have a career," Wanda said as she scanned the desk nervously for evidence of what else she might have eaten.

"Had," said the editor. "You *had* a career. Your last three books sucked, and I'm only saying that because I care. And also because they sucked. You were just phoning it in. There's no life in the series anymore. No passion."

"Ed Parsippany has been phoning it in for years," Wanda said defensively. "Trevor Dunwoody is a tired character. I mean, seriously, how many times can someone save the world before it gets old and formulaic?"

"Hundreds," said the editor. "Thousands. Look at DC Comics. Look at Marvel. Entire companies built on story after story of the same handful of characters saving the world. People can't get enough of it."

"But I don't want to write comics." It struck her suddenly that Trevor Dunwoody was just a comic book character for adults who didn't want to admit they read comics. "You know," said Wanda, "maybe readers need someone a little more nuanced than Trevor Dunwoody. Maybe the real problems in the world today don't come from dramatic supervillains and can't be solved with guns. Maybe the real problems come from people not understanding each other because they don't take the time to listen. Imagine if people truly listened and empathized and understood. Imagine what the world would be like then."

"Look, Wanda, we publish thrillers, not fantasy. Put Trevor's balls back on, stop making him cry, and get his trigger finger ready. He's got ten more people to shoot before this caper is wrapped up, and I don't want to catch him simpering or talking about feelings. Save that for your romances. Got it?"

"Yeah," said Wanda. "I got it."

She ended the call and laid her head on the desk. This is what I get, she thought. I slave away all day, all alone, for someone to tell me my work is shit. Then the voice of the editor rang through her mind. Your work *is* shit. Because you're stoned. Just follow the outline. That's all you have to do.

That was the same advice Wanda was always giving to Hannah when Hannah refused to adhere to the story line.

Wanda was surprised to feel Dirk's hand on her back. She hadn't heard him come in. He stroked the length of her spine, then began to knead her shoulders. Without taking her head off the desk, she asked, "Have you been in here the whole time?"

"Mmm hmm."

She relaxed at his touch.

"We're going out tonight," he said. "Remember?"

She wanted him to slide his hands down and press his thumbs into the muscles of her aching lower back. He did it without her saying a word, as if by instinct.

"You're tense down here," he said.

"I know."

And she knew they would get dressed up. And she knew he would be sweet and playful and charming, and the food would be good and he wouldn't care how much it cost. And she knew they would have sex. And she knew that tomorrow or the day after that, she'd hate him again. But she was low now, and he could pull her out of it. She was low, and she had nothing else in her life that could make her feel good.

She looked forward to dinner, and she didn't have to tell herself not to think about tomorrow, because she was already practiced at shutting out awareness of the bad moments to come, so they wouldn't ruin the good of the now.

10

She's back with him, Hannah thought. The fog had thickened and pressed itself against the windows of the house. She could just make out the green of a flowerless rosebush outside the window, but beyond three feet, all was gray.

She heard someone knocking about in the kitchen and knew Trevor had returned. The sound of the silverware drawer opening and closing, followed by the sound of a lid being unscrewed and dropped on the counter told her he was making a sandwich. Peanut butter. The only kind he knew how to make.

Strange he'd be hungry, she thought, after having his manhood shot off.

In a moment, he appeared in the doorway, leaning at ease against the frame as he chewed through a mouthful of food.

She knew right away he was intact. Otherwise he'd be blubbering like a four-year-old who'd just lost his favorite toy.

"How'd it go?" she asked.

He gave a thumbs up as he chewed.

"You seriously didn't—" She glanced at his crotch and then decided it wasn't something she wanted to contemplate. "You're all good?"

"All good," Trevor said.

That's strange, she thought. No one escapes what is written, and she knew what Wanda was going to write.

Hannah thought back to the state of the world just before Trevor disappeared. The fog had rolled back and the air was bright. When he left, the fog came back thick and dark. Wasn't that Wanda's anger? Wasn't that the part of her that wanted to kill Dirk? If so, she should surely have blasted Trevor's weenie off.

Or had the fog come from Wanda getting high? Had she gotten stoned and lost her resolve? She was good at losing her resolve. It's what kept her with Dirk through all those years of knowing better.

"Where's the handle?" Hannah asked.

"Huh?" Trevor was licking his fingers while he chewed the last bite of sandwich.

"The handle to pump the well?"

Trevor shrugged.

"We need it," Hannah said. "Or we'll have no water."

Trevor said, "What do normal people do?"

"What?"

"I mean, if you're not out saving the world. If you have no mission, if there's no glory to chase, what do you do?"

"Well for starters, you have to eat and drink. And that's a problem now that we can't pump water from the well. I'd say your question is moot, because we're both going to die of thirst."

"Can't you ask Wanda for some soda or something?"

"Wanda can't hear me. She's never been able to hear me. I've been stuck here for so long, I wonder if she'd even notice if I died."

"I'll see if I can rig something up," Trevor said. "Maybe there's enough wood in the basement to make a new handle."

"Well that's something right there," Hannah said. "Something you can do instead of saving the world."

Trevor sighed, wondering if this was all normal people did, if life from now on would be this mundane.

"You know, I might be stuck here too," Trevor said.

"How's that?"

"The whole plot of my novel fell apart."

"Oh," said Hannah absently. The thought of company, his company, after her long isolation didn't exactly thrill her. But something had changed about him. He seemed less charged, less consumed by his own self-importance.

"Hey, uh, thanks for the words," he said.

"Huh?" Hannah wondered how long it would be before Wanda got his plot back on track. Did it matter? One day he would be here, and then one day he wouldn't. And the world would go on that way forever, until Wanda died, or until Wanda figured out the plot of her own life, until she broke out of the cycle of fog, of hating Dirk and needing him.

His hold on her is unbreakable, Hannah thought. She knows the situation she's in. She knows what she's doing, just as surely as a junkie knows she's an addict. She just can't break out. And I can't get through to her.

"For telling me what to say to Wanda," Trevor explained.

"What? Did you say something to Wanda?" Hannah asked absently.

"Just what you told me to say. I made a vow. And Trevor Dunwoody is a man of his word." Then, with a touch of bitterness, he added under his breath, "Even if I have to live the rest of my life as a goddamn choirboy. Trevor Dunwoody is a man of his word."

The thoughts were moving quietly in her brain, the pieces coming together in slow motion.

"Trevor?" Her tone told him she was coming to an important realization.

"Huh?"

"Tell me what happened. What happened there when you found the president?"

"He had this big gun. He was going to blast me. I looked up and said the words you told me to say, and he put the gun away."

"You looked up? You said the words to Wanda?"

"Yeah."

"And she heard you?"

"I guess so. I'm here, right? All in one piece."

She thought again. In the moments before Trevor last disappeared, the world had been bright. The fog had rolled back and the grass and trees were green because something had happened. Something in Wanda's waking life had brightened this inner world and brought life back into it, and if Hannah could move her toward that thing...

"Who did you say Wanda was speaking with before you last went away? It was Dallas or Houston or something like that."

"You mean dork boy? Dweebus?"

"That's not his name."

"*You're a swell gal, Wanda,*" Trevor mocked. "*Maybe someday we can hold hands.*"

"Oh shut up," said Hannah. "Go work on a handle for the pump. I need some time to think."

As Trevor turned toward the basement stairs, Hannah said, "Do me a favor."

"What?"

"While you're working, tell Wanda to go talk to Dallas. Just keep saying it over and over while you work."

"Yeah, sure."

11

Dirk had made bacon, eggs, pancakes, and fresh coffee. The intensity of his focus as he watched her over the table made Wanda uneasy. The fact that he had made her favorite breakfast made her feel warm and loved and worried all at once. A favor like this usually indicated the beginning of a charm campaign, the narcissist's way of roping in his prey after having offended her, reeling her back and resecuring her admiration and dependence.

He was paying the toll for his offense with Shana, and Wanda was accepting the payment. He had taken her to the new French restaurant last night, and lavished on her the full power of his warmth. They came home and had sex, and they had sex again when they woke up. His favorite way to start the day, and hers too.

Normally by now, securely back in the good graces of his admirer, Dirk would have turned his attention to other things. To work perhaps, where he could puff himself up under the admiring gaze of the girls in his undergraduate class, or to the new spring suits in the clothing catalog that could make him look as dashing (he thought) as the models on the pages.

But still he looked at her, as if his work weren't done, as if he hadn't fully sucked her back into the Dirk Jaworski universe. She wanted to ask him what was wrong, but she feared provoking his temper. More than an angry eruption, she feared his cutting insults, those clever backhanded compliments targeted with uncanny precision at whatever she happened to feel most insecure about in the moment. A cruel word from him at breakfast could leave her deflated for the entire day, and she didn't want to do anything to bring it out of him. So she sat quietly and drank her coffee, balanced on the razor's edge of the happiness brought on by good sex and a special breakfast. Funny, she thought, how even my happiest moments with him are tinged with fear.

"What were you thinking of?" he asked coldly.

She knew exactly what he was asking. What had she been thinking of while they were having sex this morning? Or more to the point, *who* was she thinking of?

"That dweebus," she said, surprised at the sound of her own voice. She had meant to say, "Nothing, why?" But instead, this came out. Dweebus. Where had that word come from? She had never uttered it before.

"Austin?"

How the hell did he know who she was talking about?

"Yeah."

"You were thinking of Austin while we were having sex?" He laughed in a way that made her feel stupid and small. "Seriously?"

"I was mean to him the other night."

"When?" Dirk asked.

His tone of accusation made her feel she had done something wrong, and she replied defensively. "He came by to see you, remember? But you were out with that... Counseling that student."

"Why would you feel bad about anything that happened with Austin?" His tone was haughty. "And why would you bother thinking about it during sex?"

"I don't know," Wanda answered honestly. "I have no idea where the idea came from, or how it got in my mind."

"What did you guys do?"

"Nothing, Dirk. We just talked."

"What's the point of talking to a guy like Austin?"

"He was telling me about—"

"He probably just wanted sympathy."

"No, he—"

"He wanted you to feel bad for him because he lost his job. He wanted a pity fuck. That's what he wanted. You know he's been in love with you for years."

"You think?"

"Oh, come on!" Dirk got up from the table and set his coffee cup beside the sink. "Does it turn you on?"

"What?"

"Austin wanting you."

"I don't think he wants me in that way."

"Well what other way would he want you?" He turned on the sink and rinsed his hands.

"He likes to talk. And so do I."

"Yeah," said Dirk as he wiped his hands on a dish towel. "You're all gushy feely and he's mentally unzipping your pants."

"No, Dirk. I'm not all gushy feely. Not with him."

"Well maybe you should be," he said as he turned to leave. "You can dump all the annoying feelings on him and save the good stuff for me. He's the kind of symp who'll suck it all up like a sponge. Clean up those dishes."

"Don't talk to me like that. Fuck you, Dirk!"

"Fuck you!" he said from the hall. "When you cook, I clean. When I cook, you clean. A deal's a deal."

"Jerk!"

Damnit, Wanda thought. Why do I even care if that bastard likes me? Something is wrong with my emotional wiring.

12

"Hold it steady," Trevor said. "So the holes line up with the bracket and I can get the bolts through."

Hannah slid the heavy wooden handle up an inch until the holes lined up.

"That's not too heavy for you?" Trevor asked.

"No."

He slid the first bolt through, and then the second. Then he told her to let go.

When she wiped her hands on the satin dress, he said, "You're going to ruin that thing."

"I'm sick of it. I feel like I've been wearing it all my life, waiting for one of Wanda's heroes to carry me away."

Trevor twisted the nut onto the top bolt with his fingers.

"It doesn't suit you."

"No."

"To be honest..." He paused to twist the second nut onto the bottom bolt. "I see you in pants."

Hannah let out a little chuckle of surprise. "That's funny. You're the first person who's said that."

"I see you as more of a practical type. A get-things-done kind of person."

She was glad he said *person* and not *woman*. "You can understand, then, how I'm going crazy here."

"Oh, I get it," Trevor said as he applied the wrench to the top bolt. "Anyone would go crazy being stuck here."

"Can you ask her?"

"Ask her what?"

"Ask Wanda to put me in pants."

"Yeah, sure." He finished tightening the top bolt. As he started on the bottom bolt, he said in a low voice, "Wanda, get her out of that stupid dress and put some pants on her."

"You told her to talk to Dallas, didn't you?" Hannah asked.

"About a hundred and fifty times."

"I can tell. She's unsettled. We were having sex this morning and—"

"Wait, you were having sex? With Wanda?"

"No. Wanda was having sex with Dirk and—"

"Oh," said Trevor, less interested now. He finished tightening the second bolt. "You said *we*."

"I feel what she feels, so I can guess what she's up to, even if I can't see or hear her. She was having sex with Dirk, and she was thinking of Dallas."

"Thinking of, like... doing it?"

"No. She felt bad about something that happened between them."

"She was mean to him," Trevor said.

"Was that it?"

Trevor nodded and dropped the wrench into the wooden toolbox. "He asked for it, in my opinion. The guy's a dweeb."

"But that's a big deal. For her to think of him when she's having sex with Dirk. Even if the thoughts aren't sexual. She's always been so physically wrapped up in Dirk. This is the first time she's had room in her mind for something else. I mean, the first time during sex."

"Yeah, he felt it too," said Trevor.

"How do you know?"

"Did you hear them talking at breakfast?"

"No."

"That guy's a prick. He doesn't care how miserable she is, as long as she keeps worshipping him. And as soon as she stops, he'll find a replacement. I know his type."

Trevor pumped the handle and watched the clear water gush into the old wooden bucket.

"Keep working the Dallas angle," Hannah said. "And don't call him dweebus. It might bias her opinion." Hannah reassessed him as he lifted the water bucket. "You know, you're a lot more interesting when you're not racing around shooting people."

"Tell you the truth," Trevor said, "I needed a break."

"Well, keep talking to Wanda. We need her healthy again, so she can write us out of here."

"Hey." Trevor smiled. He nodded toward her as if to say, Look at yourself.

Hannah looked down to see herself dressed in a simple white blouse and black slacks.

"Thank God," she said.

13

For the life of her, Wanda could not understand why she had spent the entire morning on her iPad looking for open professor jobs and new houses in Dallas. She couldn't have located the city on a map or named its core industries or any famous person from there other than J.R. Ewing and the Cowboys.

It was 11:30 a.m. She wasn't stoned, and she didn't want to be. Dirk was a jerk and could clean his own damn dishes, and Austin was a dweeb, but he was a sincere dweeb, and she should apologize to him in a way that didn't lead him on. She called his cell, but it went straight to voicemail. She knew he sometimes turned it off while he worked. But he wasn't working anymore. If anything, he was packing. So why not stroll on over to his house and tell him in person that she was sorry for being a bitch?

She walked past the office on her way upstairs to get dressed. The computer monitor was dark and would stay that way because Trevor Dunwoody was not interesting enough to write about, and neither was the president or any other character Ed Parsippany had ever written, and that stupid bitch editor could shove her outline up her ass.

Forty minutes later, as she stood before the mirror applying eyeliner, she asked herself why she had showered, why she had put on fresh black slacks and a white blouse— the same outfit Hannah was wearing—and why her eyes looked so white and clear.

Because you're not stoned for once, she told herself. Your eyes look good when they're not all bloodshot. She couldn't remember the last time she'd seen them like that, or the last time she'd put on real clothes in the daylight hours. She was used to sitting in front of a monitor in sweats or tights, pouring out the contents of her imagination.

The sun was warm on the walk to Austin's. The sky was clear and blue. In a few weeks, after the students were done with finals, the moisture of the summer air would turn the sky a paler blue. The oppressive humidity would keep people indoors during the day, and the outdoor tables of the cafes would fill at night with lovers and families and intellectual college-town types talking of literature over beer and wine.

Did Dallas have outdoor cafes? Or was everyone down there too busy drilling oil wells and eating barbecue and rooting for the Cowboys?

Why did she care about Dallas anyway?

Austin's house was a small two-story craftsman, like hers, only he rented while she and Dirk owned. An adjunct professor could never afford to buy a house. Even renting, he had to share. His housemate Audrey was intimidatingly beautiful, though she had vandalized herself with poorly chosen tattoos.

There was one of a spider, and one of a butterfly, and one of a motorcycle, all done in different styles with different color palettes, a pastiche of drunken whims and contradictory moods.

For months after Austin arrived in town, Wanda wondered why he wasn't dating Audrey. They lived in the same house and they seemed to get along. He was OK looking and she was stunning. He had all the time in the world to work her, so why didn't he? Was he gay?

No. She was. Wanda saw her kissing another woman at a bar one evening, and for the next six months Audrey and Trish were always together. Too bad for Austin, Wanda thought. He had had the perfect setup, sharing the house with the lithe, intriguing beauty, and even their names went together. Austin and Audrey sounded like the couple all the other couples would measure themselves against.

This is how my mind works, she thought as she ascended the steps to Austin's house. Writing or not, this is how it churns, and the ideas aren't all bad when I'm not stoned. I should lay off the weed. It's like a weight has been lifted from my mind and—

"Is Austin here?"

"No," said Audrey, standing in the doorway with the perfect skin of her perfect arms covered with tattoos that could never match the beauty of the canvas they were drawn on. Why did she do that to herself?

"He might be back soon. Wanna come in?"

"Sure."

The scene inside the house startled her. She felt a pang of sadness at the sight of all the boxes, the piled books, the artifacts of a life waiting to be sorted into toss or keep.

"Are you moving too?" Wanda asked.

"Just three blocks," Audrey said. "In with Sandy."

Who was Sandy? I always know when Audrey has a new girlfriend, Wanda thought. Am I that out of touch that I don't even recognize the name of the lover she's going to move in with? "Oh," she said. "Congratulations."

Audrey smiled. "It's not that kind of move-in. She's straight."

"Oh." Wanda wondered whether, if she and Audrey ever lived together, they might hook up. She's so fucking beautiful, Wanda thought, if she wanted me to kiss her... But she'd have to keep her arms covered. Those tattoos! And God only knows what's on her back.

"Where did Austin go?"

"To get more boxes and tape. How have you been?"

"Oh, you know... Just writing." Just all alone writing and eating, my ass fusing to my chair. And my boyfriend is a jerk, but you know that. And I want to move to Dallas.

"You look good," Audrey said.

"I do?"

"Your eyes." Audrey motioned to her own eyes. "They're so clear and bright."

Wanda smiled.

"You want something to drink? A Coke?"

"Sure."

Wanda walked into Austin's bedroom. His was on the first floor, Audrey's was upstairs. The bed was unmade, and a pile of unwashed clothing stood atop an old red suitcase that sat open on the floor. He'll never get all that in there, she thought. And I hope he has the sense to wash it first.

A stack of textbooks sat on the printer beside the desk. Biochemistry and molecular biology. Without opening them, she knew they were filled with diagrams of molecules that connected H's and N's and C's and O's in patterns that looked like honeycombs. And there would be blurry photos from microscopes that could just as well have come from telescopes. These were the things eighteen-year-olds had learned to decipher under the tutelage of Austin Reed with his clear explanations and infinite patience.

"He just texted me," Audrey said, handing Wanda an icy glass of Coke. "He won't be back for another couple hours. He ran into a friend and they're having lunch."

"Oh."

"Anything you want me to tell him?"

"No. I just came over to apologize. I was kind of rude to him the other night."

"I know."

"Did he tell you?"

"No. But I knew what he was going over there to tell you. And I could read it on his face when he got home."

Wanda felt a tinge of shame. Not at Audrey's judgment. She didn't seem to be judging. Audrey never seemed to judge anyone. She was easygoing that way, the same way Austin was. Wanda's shame came from her own judgment of her own behavior.

"You know he really likes you," Audrey said.

"I know. I like him too. But not like that."

"Are you sure?"

"What do you mean, am I sure?" Wanda felt the question was out of line. She heard it not as, Are you sure you don't like Austin, but instead as, Are you sure you're really in love with Dirk? The question cut a little deeper coming from Audrey, whose opinion and intelligence she respected.

"It wouldn't matter if I did," Wanda asserted. "I'm in love with Jerk... Jadirk..." She couldn't get the name out. "I'm in love with Jerk Worship!" She clapped her hand over her mouth before it could let out any more words she didn't want herself to hear.

"Suit yourself," Audrey said. She turned to leave.

"I'll come back later. When is he leaving?"

"Day after tomorrow."

"Well I'll definitely say goodbye before he goes to Dallas."

"He's not going to Dallas," Audrey said from the echoing hallway. "He's going to California."

Austin... Dallas... California... Points on a map representing places that are only real to the people who live there, like ink on the printed page. Like words laid out on a page by a solitary human mind until a second mind comes along to read them, to bring them back to life, like rain reviving desiccated desert plants.

At the sight of the handwritten pages strewn across his desk, she felt a sharp pang of grief. You'll miss him, Wanda. You know you will.

But all we ever do is talk, and we can still do that on the phone.

What sorts of things did Austin write about? She didn't want to pry, but hadn't he read her writing? Surely then she could read his.

Notes about glycolysis and cellular energy production. Processes on which her life depended that seemed utterly remote and abstract. Things happening inside her body all the time of which she was unaware.

She shifted the papers and found a drawing. A sketch of a teenage boy. Austin's youngest brother. She recognized him from the photos on Austin's phone. It was a good likeness done in pencil with careful shading. Strikingly good.

Below that was another drawing. A spot-on portrait of Hannah Sharpe, the character who had no story, whose face had never seen the light of day. How could he have known?

14

Hannah paced the threadbare rug of the ancient farmhouse.

"God she's upset."

"Will you please stop pacing?" Trevor asked.

"I can't. I've never felt her so upset."

"Is she angry?"

"No."

"What is it then?"

"It's..." Hannah tried to sort it out as she paced, her arms folded tightly across her chest. Her hands stroked her shoulders as if she were trying to keep warm. The fog outside the windows had turned black. It billowed against the panes like roiling coal smoke.

"It's a kind of grief. A kind of terror." She stopped and looked at Trevor who sat at ease on the couch examining the inner workings of an old alarm clock that had no hands. "It's the kind of dread you feel when you know someone is about to die."

"What should I tell her?" Trevor asked.

"Keep pushing her toward Dallas. You have to be relentless. You have to really batter her."

"Are you sure that's healthy?"

"I don't know. But I know what's unhealthy. Dirk is unhealthy. Dirk is poison. This fog would never be so black if he hadn't poisoned her all these years with doubt and fear."

"So you want me to push her into the arms of another man?"

"He's the only thing she's got right now. And he does care about her. And she knows it."

"I don't think she has any passion for him."

"She doesn't need any more passion right now. She just needs to get out. That's the first step. From there, the world opens up. And you know what, Trevor? I trust her to do the right thing. Just keep pushing. If you can get her to drop Dirk, it'll be like cutting the anchor chain."

Trevor noticed the clock ticked when he wound it. He thought about fashioning hands for it from the wood in the basement. They would have to be small. The work would be delicate. Not the kind he was suited to.

"Will do," Trevor said.

15

"Hey, babe, run to the store and get some A1, will you?"

"Stay out of my office when I'm working, Dirk."

"Why? Do you need brainpower to write that stuff?"

"Why do we need A1?"

"Think about it for a second." His tone was condescending. "Why do people need A1? Who's that woman?" Dirk picked up the drawing that Wanda had taken from Austin's house.

She calmly took it back. "There's a bottle of A1 in the pantry."

"Aren't you supposed to refrigerate that stuff?"

"After it's open," Wanda said, putting the drawing back on her desk.

Dirk picked it up again. "Who is this?"

"I don't know, Dirk. Just leave it alone." When she tried to snatch it away from him, he pulled back, and they ripped the drawing in two.

"Damnit!" Wanda exclaimed. "Get out of here!" She hit his chest with the side of her fist and he laughed.

On his way out of the office he said, "I invited Austin."

"For what?" Wanda asked.

"For steaks and counselling," Dirk said from the hallway.

"What kind of counselling does Austin need?"

Dirk returned to the doorway. "He lost his job, remember?"

"He already has a new one."

"Where?"

"California."

"No, which university?"

"No university. It's a startup."

"Well there you go." There was something snide in his tone. Something smug and self-satisfied.

Wanda stood and faced him. "What's that supposed to mean?"

"It's kind of an admission of defeat, isn't it? He couldn't cut it in the university, so now he has to go out into the real world."

Wanda stood thinking long after Dirk left. As she listened to him rummage through the pantry—and, by the way, the A1 sauce is right in front, she thought, so why the hell are you rummaging—she considered his words. She "unpacked" them, as his professorship liked to say, to expose the underlying assumptions.

The real world and the university were two different things. Actually, two different universes, Wanda thought, each with its own set of rules. The university revered people like Dirk. They built auditoriums for him and his ilk to broadcast their pomposity to audiences of impressionable young people who paid so much money for the privilege of listening that they would be in debt for the rest of their lives.

They gave the professors power over these people. The students knew who they had to please.

Whom they had to please, Wanda corrected. Or was that the internalized voice of the Distinguished Professor of Faultless Grammar correcting her? The one who couldn't find the bottle of A1 sauce that sat front and center on the pantry shelf?

"Wandaaa!" he shouted.

When he yelled like that, she could measure the depth of his frustration by how far he stretched out the last syllable of her name. That was only three A's, she thought. He's just ramping up.

She went back to unpacking Dirk's assumptions. Now if leaving the university for the real world was an admission of defeat, something you do only if you can't cut it in the university, then the real world must be a step down from the university. In the real world, people don't get auditoriums and podiums and the forced attention of crowds of young people, crowds of inexperienced young women with firm breasts and naive ideas of love. No, the real world isn't built to glorify you, Dirk Jaworski, and it would be a real step down, wouldn't it, to have to show up to a job each day where you were expected to make a meaningful contribution.

"Wandaaaaa!"

Where you're a member of a team instead of the master of a realm, Wanda continued. Where the glory, if there is any, goes to all rather than to one. Oh, that would be a giant demotion for you now, wouldn't it, Dirk?

The rummaging sounds from the pantry had grown to a violent thrashing.

Dirk yelled "WAAAAAN…"

Uh oh, she thought. There's the pause.

"DAAAAAAAA!"

His scream had the throaty rasp of an outraged four-year-old. She closed her eyes to calm herself.

"Where the hell is the goddamn A1?"

"It's in your hand, Dirk."

"What?" He sounded surprised. "No it's not."

"Your other hand."

"Oh yeah."

It was the same story every time he looked in the pantry. If he didn't think what he was looking for was in there, he'd blindly grab the first thing on the shelf with his left hand and start digging through everything else with his right.

Now he was whistling happily as he opened the fridge. The whistling, more than the screaming, made her want to strangle him. The stupid, mindless happiness of it...

She knew how the rest of the evening would go. Dirk would put on a performance for Austin, an evening-long monologue showing off how smart he was, and Austin would sit quietly, listening now and then for the pauses during which Dirk expected to be praised or acknowledged or challenged to show even deeper erudition.

Wanda would talk to him when Dirk was out of the room. When Dirk was tending the grill or washing his hands, she and Austin would have moments of real conversation. But it wouldn't be deep or satisfying because there wouldn't be enough time during Dirk's absences, and he would always shatter their rapport when he returned. She and Austin would skim across the surface as they always did when Dirk was in the house. But it would be something. For some brief moment of the evening, another human being would see her and hear her, and she would feel through his reactions a different sense of who she was.

And if Dirk drank too much wine, they would fight before bed. And if they fought... There was only ever one ending to that story, one path to the mutual release of hostility. It was what made her hate herself and think she loved him.

She looked again at the torn drawing, smoothed it out with her palm.

Hannah Sharpe, where are you, she wondered.

16

Hannah started.

"What?" asked Trevor. "Why'd you jump?"

"She sees me."

"How do you know?"

"I just know." She turned from the window, letting go of the velvet curtain she'd been holding back to peer out at the fog. The roiling black smoke had faded to a dense light gray. Though only a little bit of light filtered down through the clouds, the fact that there was any at all told Hannah that somewhere up above was sunshine.

"Try talking to her," Trevor said. "Maybe she can hear you."

Hannah closed her eyes and thought, Wanda, you need to get out. He sucks the life out of you and you know it. You need to break away, and it has to be a violent, decisive break.

Hannah felt the shudder before Trevor heard the windows rattle.

"Whatever you said, she didn't like it."

"She knows what's going on," Hannah said. "She knows who she is and what she's doing. But it's not a question of knowing anymore, it's a question of doing. How can a person be so stuck? And why won't she listen to me?"

"I don't know," Trevor said. "My author gave me zero understanding of women. I can only undress them."

"Are you learning anything here?"

"Yeah, actually." Hannah saw a depth of knowledge in his eyes as he turned over the alarm clock in his hands. "Yeah..." He looked up at her. "To be honest, it's not very comfortable. It's not an awareness I would have asked for, to know that I've made people feel the way he makes her feel."

"But you have to learn some time."

Trevor shook his head. "Not in the world I was living in. Hey, check this out." He stood from the couch and showed her the clock. "You see these hands? You see how thin and delicate the wood is? I carved them with a penknife in the basement."

"That's nice. But what good do they do us in a world that has no time? In a world where nothing changes?"

She lifted the curtain again and looked outside. The churning fog dredged up a fragment of memory from Wanda's subconscious into Hannah's direct view: the steam from the witch's cauldron in the university theater's production of Macbeth. The lines came back to her at once, and Hannah repeated them under her breath.

Tomorrow, and tomorrow, and tomorrow,
Creeps in this petty pace from day to day,
To the last syllable of recorded time;
And all our yesterdays have lighted fools
The way to dusty death.

Trevor hadn't read Shakespeare. He thought the words were her own, and they moved him. How eloquent, he thought. The spirit of this neglected woman.

"Wanda," said Trevor. "What time is it?"

He sat quietly and listened as he wound the key on the back of the alarm clock.

"Wanda," he repeated patiently. "I need you to look at the clock and tell me what time it is."

Tick tick tick, went the clock. What does she feel, he wondered. Hannah in her timeless desolation?

"Five forty-two," said the voice.

He watched Hannah to see if she had heard it, but no. She didn't react.

"Five forty-two," he repeated. As he turned the hands, he remembered how in book three of the Trevor Dunwoody series he had blown up the terrorist's munitions factory. Trevor on a suicide mission, sneaking past dozens of guards in the dark of night. Past the infrared sensors to set the detonator. Once the bomb went, it set off all the other explosives and the whole facility, sixty thousand square feet, went up in a billowing tower of smoke and flame.

He had achieved his task, had even made it out alive, surviving the blast with only a few scrapes and burns.

But somehow, this small act of creation was more satisfying than the most spectacular acts of destruction. The tiny wooden hands he had built. The setting of the hour. Bringing time back to a place that had none.

From here, he told himself, there would be change. Time would move forward, and tomorrow would not be the same as yesterday.

He had never sat still long enough to see the Hannahs of the world.

"Wanda," he said aloud as he set the ticking clock on the end table. "Kiss the dweebus."

17

"What was that?" Dirk asked as he twisted a corkscrew into a bottle of red wine at the kitchen counter.

"What was what?"

"You just said *five forty-two.*"

"That's what time it is."

"And?" He popped the cork and poured a glass for himself.

"Didn't you just ask me the time?"

"No." Dirk tasted the wine and approved. "How much pot did you smoke today?"

"None, actually."

"And you're still hearing things?"

"Don't try to gaslight me, Dirk. You asked me clear as day what time it was, and I told you."

"Get yourself a glass," Dirk said as he walked toward the back door to light the grill.

"You could have poured one for me." Wanda opened the cabinet.

The doorbell rang and Dirk said, "Better yet, get the door."

Wanda removed two glasses from the cabinet and left them on the counter beside the wine.

She smiled when she opened the door, and was surprised at how genuine her smile was.

"Come in."

Austin handed her a package wrapped in gift paper. She could feel the frame inside the wrapping. A photo, perhaps? An eight-by-ten photo? Of what?

"Nice to see you, Wanda."

When he crossed the threshold, she heard Dirk's voice behind her.

"Kiss the dweebus!"

She turned angrily to snap at him, but he wasn't there.

She turned back to Austin. "Did you hear that?"

"Hear what?" He leaned in and smiled and whispered, "Have you been smoking Indica again?"

"No." Why am I whispering, she wondered. Because he's whispering. And I'm too close. Stay out of kissing range.

"No, I just thought I heard something. Is this for me?"

"More for Dirk."

"Oh." She couldn't hide her disappointment. Austin is moving in two days, going away forever, and after all our conversations, all the walks and lingering over late morning coffee, he comes with a gift for Dirk.

He had a bag too. A paper grocery bag with a six-pack of beer.

"I brought you something to drink," he said. He raised the bag to show her. Red Stripe. In the crumpling of the bag she heard a whisper. "Kiss the dweebus!"

God, I've been smoking way too much pot, she thought. I'm hearing things even when I'm not high. I wonder if it permanently alters the structure of your brain.

"I'll put that in the fridge," she said, taking the beer. "You want me to open one for you?"

She was already walking away when he responded. "What are you having?"

"I was going to have a glass of wine." She hoped he wouldn't say *I'll have one too.*

"I'll have one too."

She opened the fridge and started clearing room for the beer. If I told Dirk I was having wine, she thought as she slid a bottle from the six-pack, he'd say he wanted beer. She got the opener from the drawer and popped the top off. Because it doesn't matter to Dirk what I do or what anyone else does. He's not susceptible to influence in that way. He's not the kind who just caves in to the first suggestion and says, Oh I'll have what you're having.

You see, Austin, she thought, that's part of what makes you such a dweeb. Where *did* that word come from? Dirk doesn't use it. Neither does Louise. Or you. And who else do I talk to? Maybe I read it somewhere.

She held the beer out to Austin.

"I thought we were having wine."

"Well—" Wanda was about to correct him before she remembered that they had indeed agreed on wine. But now the bottle was open, and Dirk wouldn't drink it because he was out back at the grill with his own wine glass.

What the hell, she thought. She put the bottle to her lips and took a long swig.

"Actually, beer sounds good," Austin said. "I'll have one too."

God, you dweeb!

At least he had the decency to open the fridge and get it himself. Dirk would have asked her to do it. Actually, no. Dirk wouldn't have asked because he didn't have to anymore. She would simply have done it, understanding that that was what he expected.

Funny what I notice when I'm not stoned.

She lingered on the thought for just a second, but it was long enough for him to kiss her with his cold lips, with his lips as cold as hers that had just come off the top of the beer bottle.

She pushed him away. "Jesus, Austin, what the fuck?"

"You know what, Wanda. I told you, even though I didn't have to. You've known for years."

"Dirk is right outside."

"Dirk is a prick."

"You come in here, come into Dirk's house and kiss his girlfriend? What kind of friend are you?"

"I came into *your* house, Wanda. And I kissed *you*."

"You better back the fuck off. In fact, why don't you just leave? Just get out."

"You'll never see me again," Austin said.

"I'll come and say goodbye before you leave town," she said. The words stung her more deeply than they stung him.

"No you won't."

"I will, Austin. I do care about you. I do."

"But you're going to the beach in the morning."

"No I'm not."

"Yes you are."

"How do you know?"

"Dirk posted it on Facebook."

"What?" She picked up her phone from beside the sink. "Why didn't he tell me?"

"Because he doesn't think of you."

"Well…" She paused while she pulled up Dirk's page. "Obviously he meant it as a surprise. He *can* be romantic."

"A surprise?" Austin asked. "Posted on Facebook? Announced to all your friends but not to you?"

Wanda stared at the screen. "Huh. Louise Pennypacker says the water is surprisingly warm for spring. And she's pretty sure Peter is the dad."

"What's that supposed to mean?"

"Never mind."

The back door burst open to announce Dirk's entrance.

"Well well well, if it isn't my favorite ex-professor." His wine glass was empty and his teeth were purple. "Academic outcast and private-sector employee-to-be. What's shaking in your world, Austin?"

"I was just kissing your wife."

"She's not my wife. And she wouldn't kiss the likes of you, but that was a good comeback." He crossed the kitchen in a few easy strides and reached between them to open the fridge. "Step aside you two, the man of the hour has to tenderize the steaks before they go on the fire."

Dirk slid the plate of steaks from the fridge and set them on the counter. "Open one of those beers for me, will you?" He removed a heavy wood cutting block from a cabinet near the sink and slammed it dramatically on the counter, as if he were performing on stage and he wanted to be sure the people in the balcony could hear what he was doing.

Wanda pursed her lips as she removed a beer from the fridge, giving Austin a pointed look that said OK, he *is* a jerk. A point for you. Take it with grace.

He did.

Wanda opened the beer as Dirk rummaged through a drawer of odd utensils in search of the aluminum mallet with the spikey surface for tenderizing meat.

"Where's the…" He rummaged more violently, trying to think of the name of the thing he was looking for. "Where's the thing I use to pound my meat?"

"Left hand," Wanda said.

He looked and there it was.

"Oh yeah."

Wanda turned to Austin. "Hey, come in my office for a second. I want to ask you something."

18

Hannah stood at the window of the old Victorian farmhouse, watching the churning fog.

"What do you hear?" she asked.

"Well, they're talking," said Trevor.

"How's it going? What's your sense?"

"I can't tell."

"I can't either."

"She was about to kick him out, but she didn't."

"Well that's something," Hannah said. "What are they saying now?"

"Nothing. They're going to her office. Oh, and his name is Austin, not Dallas."

"She's walking close to him. Closer than usual."

"You can see that?" Trevor asked.

"No. I can feel it."

19

"What is this?" Wanda held the two halves of the drawing out to Austin.

"You took that? You took that from my desk?"

"Who is she?"

Austin took the two halves and tried to fit them together.

"Huh?" Wanda demanded. "Who is she?"

Austin shook his head. He didn't want to answer.

"An old girlfriend?"

His lips clamped shut to say he wasn't going to talk.

"Why won't you tell me? Are you in love with her? Is this someone you stalk?"

He shook his head silently.

"Why won't you tell me?"

"What do you care?"

"I'm curious who she is," Wanda said.

Austin shook his head again, looking sheepish this time.

"What?" asked Wanda.

"I'd be embarrassed."

"You'd be embarrassed to tell me about a woman in a drawing? After you just tried to kiss me in the kitchen?

After you kissed me with NO WARNING, with your cold beer lips while Dirk was right outside? NOW you're embarrassed?"

Austin took a deep breath and let it out. "Do you remember the first time we spoke?"

"You asked me that the other night," Wanda said impatiently.

"We spoke for over an hour—"

"Get to the point."

"—but I had never seen you."

"And?"

"And I drew that. That was what you looked like in my mind."

Wanda stared at him in wonder, and he felt foolish.

"That's... That's the person I saw after listening to you speak."

He dropped the papers on the desk, the image of her as she understood herself, torn in two by the struggle between her and Dirk.

"Wandaaaa!"

"What the fuck do you want, Dirk?"

"What kind of vegetables go with steak?"

20

Hannah, standing at her window, felt a sharp pang in her heart. Trevor saw the effect of it so clearly he instinctively stood to help her. She held her stomach as he guided her to the couch.

"You going to puke?" Trevor asked.

She sat.

"What did he say to her?" Hannah asked.

"I don't know," Trevor replied. "He was talking quietly. I couldn't hear him."

"Whatever it was, it really got to her. Oh, I feel sick." She bent forward as if her stomach was cramping.

"Is there anything I can get you?"

She shook her head. The fog outside darkened and billowed against the rattling windows. Trevor waited for the noise to stop, but it didn't.

"Are there earthquakes here?"

"If there are," Hannah said, "there will be one tonight. She's cracking because she's finally admitting to herself that the guy who really gets her isn't the one she's with. That her great project with Dirk, for all its passion, is a failure. That hurts. It hurts more deeply than she can say.

She sees it in the contrast between Dirk and Austin. One of them touches her where she wants to be touched. Emotionally, I mean. The other bullies his way into her feelings, and she lets him."

Hannah rocked in pain as the dishes in the kitchen rattled on the shelves.

"But she's holding on, Trevor. Holding on to the life she knows isn't working. She's stubborn as hell and she doesn't want to give in. She'll kill me before she'll do what she knows is right."

"What should I say? Tell her to kiss him?"

"She hasn't got the courage for that. Just tell her to stay near him."

"That's it?"

"That's it."

"So we leave it up to him to make the move?"

Hannah doubled over as a violent tremor shook the house. "No. She already made the call. She just doesn't know it."

She winced as a pain went through her gut, then looked up at him with difficulty.

"She has tremendous intuition," Hannah said. "She doesn't listen to it, but I feel it. I understand every bit of what it tells me. Austin is far more subtle and determined than you know. Than even he knows. But she gets it. She knows him as deeply as he knows her. She's just not consciously aware of it. She made up her mind when she chose not to throw him out after that clumsy kiss."

"You look awful," Trevor said. "Are you sure there's nothing I can do?"

"Just encourage her to sit by him, to look at him, to listen to him. Dirk's spell doesn't work on her if she's not paying attention. Keep her focused on Austin."

21

Wanda prepared asparagus and salad to go with the steak, having correctly interpreted Dirk's question *What kind of vegetable goes with steak?* to mean *Start making some vegetables to go with the steak.*

She trimmed the bottoms of the stalks and tossed the asparagus in oil, then turned them over to Dirk for grilling. That was a process in which no one was permitted to interfere, not even with helpful suggestions, because Dirk felt that other peoples' incorrect ideas contaminated his own correct ones and caused him to drop asparagus through the grill.

Wanda watched him through the screen door as she chopped the lettuce. Austin stood beside her, slicing carrots.

"You know he bought that apron just for today," Wanda said.

"Really?" Austin glanced out at Dirk in his bright white apron and towering chef's hat.

"He throws aprons away when they get stained."

"Isn't that what aprons are for?" Austin pushed the carrots from the cutting board to a plate.

"Dirk has to dress for his role, and he won't accept a second-rate costume. I told him no one wears a chef's hat when they barbecue and he said, 'Excuse me? I do.' I think he likes that it makes him look taller."

She dumped the lettuce in the bowl and picked up the plate of carrots. Austin, moving toward the fridge, put his hand on the small of her back to keep her from backing into him.

"You want a beer?" he asked.

"How about a glass of wine?"

"Wine it is."

He went the other way toward the wine bottle, brushing her shoulder on the way past, again to remind her of where he was, so she wouldn't back into him.

She read his touches differently. "Dirk's right outside, you know."

"Mmm hmm." Austin poured wine into one of the glasses Wanda had left on the counter. "He's busy too. Putting on a show." Austin pointed through the side window to the women on the back deck of the neighboring house. Though none of them were looking at him, Dirk gyrated his hips suggestively as he salted the steaks, just so that when someone did look, he would make an impression.

"Crap," said Wanda as she received the wine glass. "When he does that stupid salt dance he stops paying attention to the actual salt. Be sure to scrape both sides of your steak before you eat it, so you don't get a sodium-induced coronary."

Don't look at him, whispered a voice. *Don't look at Dirk.*

Wanda turned and looked at Austin. "Did you say something?"

"No. But hey, stop looking at Dirk for a minute. Get the cucumber and red onion. I'll show you how to make a good dressing."

The two of them stood side by side. She watched as he cut the onion into thin, even slices, quartered them, and put them in the bowl. His movements had a grace and precision that Dirk's lacked.

"Now the cucumber," he said. He peeled off most of the skin, leaving strips of dark green here and there. "Too much skin makes it tough. A little adds flavor and texture."

This was the kind of nuance that Dirk, for all his nitpicking, was incapable of understanding. Dirk saw all the details and none of the meaning. When he read Shakespeare, all he saw was the punctuation.

Austin dropped the sliced cucumbers into the bowl.

"You see that," he said. "The contrast between the bright orange carrots, the purple-red onions, and pastel green cucumber? I can name all the chemicals that produce those colors, but it's a lot more satisfying just to look at them."

She was standing close to him. Very close. She had been for some time, but why hadn't she noticed until now?

Standing that close to Dirk made her uneasy. Dirk was a threatening figure. First, he made her tense, and then he manipulated her tension. He could turn it easily into another kind of agitation, a sexual agitation in which the discomfort grew and grew until they did something to annihilate it. But it was discomfort she felt around Dirk, and it was discomfort that he exploited. She had known this for a long time, but was just now putting it into words and examining it.

She closed her eyes and tried to imagine cooking side by side with Dirk, but she couldn't. She and Dirk were like magnets. Whenever they were near each other, they were powerfully pulled together or just as powerfully pushed apart. There was no comfort around him, no comfort in her own home or in her own skin. She had let him take that away from her.

She leaned against Austin's shoulder, her eyes still closed, and whispered, "Please don't leave."

The stretching of the spring on the screen door preceded the loud slap of the door against the side of the house.

"Wandaaaa!"

"What, Dirk? What the hell is wrong now?"

"Stupid bird shit on my apron! Where's the other one?"

"Hanging on the hinge of the pantry door."

He pulled the soiled apron over his head as he stomped by and flung it on the floor.

"You're not going to leave that there," she said.

He kicked it into the air and it settled on the back of a chair.

He really is a child, she thought. And when he gets like that, I try to soothe him, like it's *my* problem. I would have helped him if Austin wasn't here.

Dirk pulled on the new apron and went back outside. A little cheer went up from the women on the deck next door as the performer re-entered the stage with a fresh costume. He took a bow, only half in jest.

Now he was saying something to the women, twirling the spatula, making some joke. The kind his eighteen-year-old students would find witty. She didn't have to look at him or hear his words to know this. She just knew.

"For the dressing," Austin said, "olive oil, vinegar, pepper, and mustard. Stone ground mustard, not the yellow kind."

She helped him gather the ingredients.

"Pour in the oil first," he said.

"Me?"

"Yeah, you."

"How much?"

"As much as three people would need."

"Well how much is that?" she asked.

"Use your judgment."

She poured in a couple of ounces, thinking about the precise instructions Dirk would have given. Everything measured out to the milliliter. All operations performed in the order of the written instructions while he hovered to correct her errors.

Two ounces didn't look like enough. She poured in one more, knowing she didn't need to look to Austin for approval.

There is no coloring outside the lines for Dirk Jaworski, she told herself as she tossed in another dash. Or I should say, for Dirk's girlfriend.

Dirk himself was a great improviser when he performed in front of an audience. His instincts came to life as he fed off the attention of the crowd. Aside from a few canned jokes here and there, there was no script. There was no crimping his style. He had to be free to follow his whim, while she, home alone without an audience, had already internalized the precise instructions that applied to *her*. She rarely deviated or transgressed. She had grown so accustomed to her straitjacket she was no longer conscious of it until now that it was off, and she felt strangely unprotected without it.

What had Ed Parsippany's editor said? That her last three books sucked. That she was just phoning it in.

Well I was, Wanda admitted. I was. There's no soul in my writing because I don't live anymore. Because my spirit is trapped and my life is stale and all I can do is to keep on doing the same old thing. Same fight with Dirk. Same resolution. Same plot in my books. Nothing changes.

The vinegar was next. Austin didn't tell her how much. He just watched. She whisked in the mustard, then fresh-ground pepper. Too little at first. A taste, and then four more twists of the peppermill.

She dipped her finger in, then licked it. "Taste," she said.

This is where the hero does something provocative and sexy, she thought. Coats his finger with the tangy dressing, with that pepper that gives it a kick, and the smooth lubricating oil, and then he sticks it in my mouth for a taste and draws it out slowly as we stare into each other's eyes.

Austin wasn't her hero.

He put his own finger to his own mouth. All he offered was a smile of approval. Simple and genuine, comfortable and familiar, like home.

She tried not to show how sad she felt at the awareness that simple smile aroused in her, at how that glimpse of home reminded her that she had been living for years in exile from herself.

Where is Hannah, she wondered. What have I done with her?

Maybe she couldn't hide it. Maybe he saw the flash of sadness. Maybe that was why he kissed her.

It wasn't the swoon-inducing hero's kiss that came on page ninety of all her novels. It was short and simple, matter of fact, an ordinary exchange between two people utterly at ease with each other.

22

"His hands," Trevor whispered as he sat on the couch. "What do his hands look like?"

He paused, breathing quietly. Then, in a barely audible whisper, "What do you see in his eyes?"

"Look," said Hannah as she paced the rug. "The fog."

It had thinned to the point where the daylight was almost bright enough to cast shadows.

"How's your stomach?" Trevor asked.

"Better. Keep working her. Quietly, subtly, like you're doing. Don't push too hard, but don't let the pressure off either. Not even for a second."

23

Dirk had gotten up from his place at the head of the table and was giving a lecture. He was halfway through the second bottle of Cabernet, which was two glasses too far for him. Every time he got drunk on wine, he fell in love with himself all over again, and now he was standing at the far end of the room with a stack of his students' papers, reading aloud their mistakes.

"*If I was to do it over again*," he read, then paused dramatically, like Hamlet contemplating the slings and arrows of outrageous fortune.

"*If I WAS to do it all over again*," he repeated, emphasizing the gravity of the grammatical error.

He slammed the paper roughly against his knee so that it made a jarring slap.

"The public school system," he thundered, "has failed to teach an entire generation the proper use of the subjunctive mood. Would anyone like to venture a guess as to how that sentence should be written?"

Austin and Wanda sat side by side at the table. "Does he want us to answer?" Austin whispered.

Wanda shook her head. "He doesn't even know we're here. He's just rehearsing for next semester."

She felt a little thrill as Austin took her hand beneath the table.

"You hardly touched your steak," she said.

"If I WERE to do it all over again," Dirk announced. "Were!" He stood with his back to them, hands on hips in an angry stance, looking up as if he were talking directly to God.

"Didn't you like it?" Wanda asked. "The steak?"

Austin nodded. "I did, but..." He put his other hand to his stomach and whispered, "Butterflies."

"You too, huh?"

It impressed her that he admitted it. Dirk didn't discuss uncomfortable feelings, particularly those that hinted at vulnerability. It was an unspoken rule in the house, one she had adopted unconsciously. She hid her feelings from him as much as she could, but he always knew. He'd come sniffing like a badger and root them out, and the fact that he could successfully force her to confess the emotions she had worked so hard to hide made her feel ashamed. Ashamed of normal human feelings that Austin admitted openly.

"WERE," Dirk thundered. "Not was. 'Was' is indicative, but we're in speculation here. And which mood do we use for speculative constructions?"

He's very sweet, Wanda thought as he squeezed her hand. I do think he gets me. But he's—

Austin leaned in and kissed her before she could finish the thought.

—not assertive enough.

Do that again, said her eyes. Harder. Like you mean it.

He did. His tongue inside her mouth was shockingly arousing.

But it's only because he's doing it right in front of Dirk, she thought. It's only because of the danger factor.

He kissed her a third time. This time she put her tongue in his mouth.

My heart's going to beat right out of my chest, she thought.

She pushed him away.

"The subjunctive!" Dirk announced dramatically, turning at last to face them. "When we speculate, we use the subjunctive mood!"

He paused, annoyed at not having the full attention of his audience.

"Excuse me," said Wanda. She wiped her mouth and got up to use the bathroom.

"Something wrong with the steaks?" Dirk asked, noticing how little Austin and Wanda had eaten.

"Butterflies," Austin said.

Dirk spun dramatically on his heel and pressed his face to the window.

"Where?"

24

"This is going better than I could have imagined," Hannah said, her face bright with hope.

She glided to Trevor, who sat quietly focused on the couch. She knelt and took his face between her hands and kissed his cheek. "You're doing a brilliant job." She beamed. "Brilliant."

She went to the window and looked out. The fog had receded a hundred yards from the edge of the house. New buds had appeared on the rosebush, on the rhododendrons, and the magnolia.

"The fog," she said brightly. "It has a different quality, doesn't it? Have you ever seen it so light?"

"Hannah," said Trevor. The sharpness of his tone told her something was wrong.

"What?" The smile left her face. "What is it?"

"She's in the bathroom."

"She's overwhelmed. I can feel it."

"I know. I think this is too much for her."

"What do you..." She trailed off at the scent of smoke drifting in through the window cracks.

"Oh no! Wanda, no!" She banged her fists against the glass. "No, no, no! Now is not the time to numb yourself."

"Maybe we took it too fast," Trevor said.

"Wanda, you need to be present. Please don't do this! Please, Wanda! Please."

25

She hadn't planned to. She had gone to the upstairs bathroom in part because she needed to pee, and in part because her own feelings had taken her by surprise and she needed time to compose herself.

The joint was on the counter by the sink. The half-smoked joint streaked with sticky brown resin. She picked it up out of habit and lit it before sitting on the toilet.

Austin Reed, she thought, you are much bolder than I ever gave you credit for.

She blew a thick column of smoke up toward the ceiling fan. Dirk didn't like the smell lingering in the bathroom.

I didn't think you could ever turn me on, but you did. She clamped the joint between her lips and pulled a few sheets of paper off the roll. Congrats on that, Austin.

She stood and flushed and took another big hit, and thought, You know, I'm actually embarrassed. She blew the smoke into the exhaust fan. Embarrassed to see myself. To see my own life so clearly. How screwed up it all is. How pathetic and predictable.

Another hit. Big exhale.

And I could tell Austin that. I could tell him I'm embarrassed and ashamed, and he wouldn't judge me. He's seen me these past two years. He's been in this house a hundred times, and he's never judged me. Not once. I've never felt an ounce of shame around him.

One more hit, and the remains of the joint went into the toilet.

You had me on edge, Austin. But now I'm relaxed.

On her way to the sink, she thought what a shame it was that he had waited until the final hour to make his move. He could have broken her and Dirk up years ago with a kiss like that. But he would have had to repeat it, ten or twenty or a hundred times to drive the point home. To let her know for sure, for absolute sure, that it was safe to jump ship. That there was another life out there that was sustainable and decent and happy.

But you waited too long, Austin. You couldn't get your nerve up until the final buzzer was about to sound.

God, this pot makes me cynical.

She washed her hands and splashed water on her face.

And it makes my eyes really bloodshot. No wonder Dirk says I look like shit.

When she opened the door, she could hear them downstairs.

"No," Dirk said loudly, "tell me what was wrong with the steak."

"There was nothing wrong with it."

"Then why didn't you eat it?"

Wanda made her footsteps loud on the wooden stairs to interrupt their argument, to tell them to put aside their disagreement and behave themselves.

"I just wasn't that hungry," Austin said.

"Dude, those steaks cost nineteen dollars a pound and I fucking slaved over that grill. Why would you come over in the first place if you weren't hungry?"

Dirk could be intensely unpleasant when he was drunk, when the alcohol stripped off the veneer and showed the selfishness of his character. Wanda paused at the bottom of the stairs, not wanting to see him.

"You invited me, remember?" Austin said. "This is our last time hanging out. I'm moving across the country."

"Yeah, well you should have stayed home if you weren't hungry."

"Lighten up," Austin said. "You can eat the leftovers for breakfast."

"Me? Eat *your* leftovers?"

"It'll help your hangover."

"You saying I'm drunk?"

Wanda wanted to walk in and separate them but she dreaded the confrontation.

"You are drunk," Austin said. "You're even more of an ass when you drink."

"And you don't need a drink to be an ass," Dirk said.

She heard silverware fall on the table. Dirk must be picking up the plates in his clumsy drunken way. Better to go in now, before it gets worse.

She put on her happiest face as she rounded the corner from the stairs.

"You two," she scolded.

Austin could see she was stoned. Wasted stoned. Her eyes were red and puffy. She was in that state he'd seen her in so many times, where she could barely put two thoughts together. She must have just smoked. She was only gone a few minutes. Her stupor would deepen as the drug made its way through her bloodstream to the receptors in her brain. He knew he couldn't reach her in that state. He knew the night was lost.

She could see the disappointment in his face. She could feel the hope rush out of him all at once. She felt ashamed for letting him down, and in a second, the shame was drowned in a flood of anger.

Don't you make me feel that way, she thought as she turned and ran up the stairs. Don't you ever put that hurt on me. I expect it from *him*, but not from you. I never expected *you* to make me feel any goddamn worse than I already do.

Locked in the bathroom, rocking back and forth on the edge of the tub, she said, God I'm sorry. I'm sorry I fucked it up, Austin, but this is who I am. I step one inch out of my comfort zone and then go running back to safety. Back to pot and Dirk and everything familiar. You cut too close tonight. Too fucking close, and I'm sorry I'm not all you thought I was, but I'm just not.

She heard the front door of the house slam. Austin was gone and Dirk was pounding at the bathroom door. "Open up, I gotta take a dump!"

"FUCK YOU!"

The scream was so loud and shrill, it took the skin off her throat.

26

"That didn't go well," Trevor said.

Hannah shook her head. "No."

"Did you know?"

"That she was ready to explode?" Hannah nodded. "This has been years in the making. The only reason she's stayed with him this long is because she has her fantasyland to escape to. The novels with their perfect heroes and happily-ever-afters. She keeps writing the same book over and over again. But she shouldn't just be living it in her imagination. If that's what she truly wants, she should be living it in real life."

"And the pot?" Trevor asked.

"People take aspirin to ease their physical pain," Hannah said. "Psychic pain requires other measures. What's your read on her?"

"She's a mess."

"You think she'll make it?"

"I don't know. What do you think?"

Hannah shrugged.

"So, what's next?" Trevor asked.

"I don't know. I don't think there's anything more we can do. It's on her now. Everything is up to her."

"That scare you?"

It wasn't the question that surprised Hannah so much as her immediate gut response. She hesitated a moment to second-guess it, but there it was, the simplest answer in the world.

"No."

27

"Are we past our little meltdown?"

That was vintage Dirk. A compassionate question posed in a belittling tone.

Wanda watched from the edge of the tub as Dirk stood at the mirror rubbing cream into his face. He had one cream for his forehead and another for the corners of his eyes. A third cream firmed up the skin beneath the eyes, and then there was a general facial moisturizer that didn't go on until after his morning shave so it wouldn't get caught in his stubble.

He turned and looked at her. "I asked you a question."

"I thought you had to use the toilet."

"Yeah, well I missed my window of opportunity because *somebody* wouldn't open the door."

Of course he had all those creams. He was the star of his own life, and everyone else's life as well, and he had to look the part.

"Why didn't you use the downstairs bathroom?"

Wanda had a bottle of body lotion for the dry winters, and a facial cleanser to try to counteract what the junk food did to her skin, but beyond that, she had stopped taking care of her appearance. Even in the early days of their relationship, she was never as attentive to her looks as he was to his.

"The downstairs toilet seat lost its veneer," he said as he carefully rubbed the corners of his eyes until the cream was no longer visible. "It chafes me."

"How do you think I feel?" Wanda asked. "I sit on it more than you do."

"Then why don't you fix it?"

Normally that remark would have steamed her. That would be the first to set her temper off. She'd snap at him, and he'd reply coolly, a cutting retort delivered with apparent indifference. That would send her temper up another notch, and so they'd begin. It might take two minutes to make him lose his temper, or it might take twenty, but it would happen, and as the conflict escalated she would feel danger, arousal, and despair. Passion was all three of those wrapped up in one neat package.

Dirk picked up the lotion for his forehead, looked at it, and put it back down.

He wants to have sex, she thought. He knows I hate the smell of that lotion, the greasiness, and if he puts it on I won't kiss him.

What did he say last time I objected to that stuff? *Just turn around. You don't have to face me when we do it.*

The thought of him revolted her. How could he want to have sex tonight? After the evening had ended so badly, with he and Austin fighting and her locking herself in the bathroom and screaming?

Did anything turn him off?

"You gonna put on your PJ's?" he asked as he loaded paste onto his toothbrush.

"I don't know."

What if I just watch him, she thought. What if I just watch him the way I watched Austin? Register the details but don't react.

But you did react to Austin, she told herself. You reacted strongly. Much more strongly than you would have guessed.

That's because he's nice, and a little kindness goes a long way in the heart of a person who's not used to getting any.

It sobered her to think of herself that way.

"Put on the green ones," Dirk said through a mouthful of foam. "The pale greens. You know how they turn me on."

He knew she was annoyed with him and wouldn't want to put those on. He waited for her refusal, waited to gauge the level of hostility roiling her heart and clouding her mind.

"OK," she said simply. "Whatever you want."

Well that was no fun. No fun for Dirk Jaworski who needed an emotional reaction to remind himself how much he mattered.

Wanda went out to the bedroom and changed while Dirk finished brushing his teeth. He spent a few minutes flossing, flashing his teeth in the mirror several times in a grin that reminded Wanda of a monkey. He did it not in search of missed food, but simply to admire the whiteness of his teeth.

"You just going to stand there in the doorway watching me?" he said. He had a way of asking questions that made them sound like commands.

"Yeah."

He dropped the floss on the counter—Wanda would clean it up in the morning—and poured a shot of mouthwash into the cap of the bottle.

He gargles like an ass, Wanda thought. He thinks he has to do it loud enough for the neighbors to hear.

Dirk spat dramatically into the sink, spattering the faucet, the counter, and the mirror in his carelessness. More work for Wanda tomorrow.

"Take off your clothes, Dirk." There was no emotion in her voice.

"Really?"

She knew that would surprise him.

"Yeah."

He pulled his shirt over his head. "Don't you need me to warm you up first?" He had the chest and shoulders of a man who spent many hours at the gym.

"What's that got to do with anything?" Wanda asked. "Can't I serve you just as well if—"

Dirk's pants and underwear came down in one quick jerk.

"Whoa!" said Wanda. "You don't waste any time, do you?"

"You're totally turning me on," he said.

"Take them off. All the way."

He did, and as she stood for a moment appraising him, her silence confused him.

"Well?" he said at last. His tone reminded her of the impatient customers she had waited on in restaurants during college summers. The ones who simply couldn't understand why she didn't jump to serve them.

"You're a fine specimen of a man," she said coolly. "But I don't like you."

She turned and left.

"Where are you going?" Dirk demanded.

"Away." She pulled on a pair of shoes and ran toward the top of the stairs, afraid he would catch her from behind.

"Come back here!"

On the third step, she felt his hand swipe at her hair.

She took the remaining steps in twos, then cut hard to the right toward the front door.

"What are you doing, you crazy bitch?"

The door didn't budge when she twisted the knob. She had to turn the deadbolt, and by then he had caught her by the waist.

She turned quickly. He would expect a blow, so instead she spat in his face. That surprised him enough to let go. In a second she was out the door, down the steps, full stride toward the sidewalk.

He was still after her when she rounded the corner.

"You're in your pajamas!" Dirk yelled. "Where are you going?"

"I don't know!"

She really didn't.

Dirk made it another half block before realizing he was naked.

He stopped and watched her run.

"Crazy fucking bitch," he muttered.

He walked slowly back to the house, looking for lights in windows, signs of wakefulness in the houses where he knew young women lived. Dirk Jaworski was putting on a free show, a free show of a fine specimen of a man, and it would be a shame if no one were there to witness it, no sleepless gawker to pick up the phone and tell a friend, "You won't believe what I just saw."

28

She marched with her arms folded across her chest, guided unconsciously toward her destination. In ten minutes she was knocking at Austin's door.

Audrey answered. "He's not here." On her lovely bare arms, the spider and the butterfly and the motorcycle looked like random graffiti.

"Do you know where he is?"

"He came back and then he left."

Wanda looked back at the street. "His car's here. Maybe he walked to the store."

"He took a Lyft. The only time he ever does that at night is when he's going out drinking. What happened between you two?"

"I don't know," Wanda said. "I honestly don't know. But how did you know something happened? Did he say anything?"

"He didn't have to."

"Was he upset?"

"Very. You know how he feels about you." Audrey hesitated as if wondering whether she had said too much. "I mean, you know now, don't you?"

"I know," said Wanda.

"And I'm sorry, but—" Audrey cut herself off, but Wanda knew what she was going to say. She knew how Audrey felt about Dirk.

"I don't want to get into your business," Audrey said. "You're a grown woman."

Coming from Audrey, whom she admired (except for the tattoos), that stung almost as much as one of Dirk's backhanded compliments.

"You want to come in and wait?"

"No," Wanda said. But she did want to come in and wait, and maybe fall asleep in the living room and not have to wake up in her own house the next morning, in her own life with the selfish narcissistic manipulating oaf who brightened and ruined all her days.

"I'll tell him you stopped by." Audrey shut the door.

Wanda walked aimlessly for the next few hours, not wanting to go home and not knowing where else to go. At 1:30, she passed a pack of leering fraternity boys on their way out of a bar. One of them turned to check her out from behind as she passed. "Well look who's ready for bed!" He stretched out his words in a mocking, suggestive tone. She remembered that she was wearing the pale green pajamas that Dirk loved to peel off of her. The frat boys' energy was the same as Dirk's, lewd and self-satisfied, but less polished, less aware of how to find and push her buttons.

The boys were merely crude and ineffective where he was instinctively accurate. He could make her come to him, even against her will at times. These kids couldn't have gotten to her through any means other than brute force, and there were four of them, she thought, and they were drunk. She crossed her arms and stepped up her pace. She didn't think about where she was going, only that she had been so stoned and so upset these past few hours that she hadn't recognized the degree to which she'd put herself at risk.

At 1:53, she was back at Austin's. The house was dark, so she rang the bell.

Audrey in her tank top, shaking her head. "He hasn't come home."

Wanda turned and left. Why didn't she ask me to stay this time, she wondered. Can't she see I'm upset? Can't she see I'm suffering?

But you already told her no, Wanda reminded herself. She asked earlier if you wanted to come in and wait, and you said no. That's pretty damn clear, isn't it? No means no, right?

Funny, she thought as she criticized herself, how one part of me, one voice can be so big, and yell and scream and make the rest of me feel so small.

And I'm so tired. I am so, so, so, so tired.

The pot had worn her down. The beer and wine and the heavy steak. The confusion at her own response to Austin's kiss. The overly long day had worn her down. The years with Dirk, years of trying to maintain a sense of self-respect while fighting battles she could never win. For Dirk, there was no losing. Simply getting her to fight was winning, and he could draw her in every time.

She climbed the steps wearily, took her shoes off on the porch, opened the door quietly. She waited at the foot of the stairs, not daring to turn on the light. When the sound of his gentle snoring drifted down, she walked silently to the sink and filled a glass of water. She drank it down, crossed the room, collapsed on the couch, and reflected on how, after so many nights like this and so many fights, exhaustion had become a state of being.

And tomorrow they wouldn't talk about it. Tomorrow they would greet each other as if nothing had happened.

The tension would remain, and the fight would resume at some point in the day, with a new subject, but it would be the same fight, and he would push her down and down and down, almost to the breaking point, and then he'd lift her up to a point of near-normalcy that felt like ecstasy compared to the depths she'd been in. And that would feel like love.

That would be tomorrow. Just like all of the tomorrows of all the yesterdays of the past six and a half years.

Tomorrow and tomorrow and tomorrow creeps in this petty pace from day to day, to the last syllable of recorded time...

Unless there is no tomorrow, she thought.

She closed her eyes.

I was too young when he found me.

Take him and cut him out in little stars...

How had Juliet's infatuation come to this?

And he will make the face of heaven so fine...

Please don't let there be another tomorrow.

...that all the world will be in love with night and pay no worship to the garish sun.

Why did he have to find me?

She tried to pray, but she was so tired she didn't know what to ask for anymore. Her own words failed her, but the words of the poet did not. She found herself muttering Romeo's speech of resignation as she sank into the couch.

Here will I set up my everlasting rest, and shake the yoke of inauspicious stars from this world-wearied flesh.

And when mercy found her it was sleep.

29

Trevor sat on the couch listening to the clock tick, the alarm clock that was now keeping time with Wanda's world. 2:33. After hearing her final whisper, he was grateful for the silence, relieved to hear her quieted.

"She's beginning to dream," Hannah said from the other end of the couch, where she was thoughtfully twisting a Rubik's cube.

"Where'd that come from?" Trevor asked.

"All kinds of things show up in her subconscious. You'd be surprised."

"You're very calm," Trevor said. "For all that's going on right now."

"I know." She gave the cube a twist and showed him that two sides of the puzzle were now complete.

"Everything that happens up there," she said, pointing up to indicate the world of consciousness, "is set up down here first. The fact that I'm calm means she's figured it out. She doesn't know it yet. Not consciously. But she's just a step away."

"What will she dream about?"

"I don't know." Hannah turned her attention back to the puzzle. "I don't always get to see her dreams, but I feel them."

30

Wanda was at sea in the jaws of a great white shark.

It could have bitten her in half, could have pulled her under with the cold, indifferent efficiency for which the species is reviled and feared. But this one was content to keep her in its grip, to thrash now and then so its teeth sunk in, to descend for sixty or ninety seconds at a time while she held her breath, returning her to the surface just as she felt her lungs would burst.

In the dream world, there was no time. In the dream world, she had existed always and forever in those fearful jaws.

Now a man was approaching in a small skiff. It was Austin in his bland khakis and faded polo shirt.

Where does he even find such boring clothes, she wondered as the shark asserted its power with a violent shake. She punched its nose to anger it, and it shook again, harder this time.

The skiff plodded on steadily through the waves. The shark didn't seem to notice its approach.

When he reached her a few seconds later, Austin said, "Climb in." He said it simply, matter-of-factly, like he was picking her up from an errand.

"Goddamnit, Austin, I can't just climb in. He's got his teeth in me."

"Grab the side," Austin said. "Pull yourself up." The ease of his tone infuriated her.

"I can't just *pull myself up*. I'm fucking dying, you asshole!"

He patted the gunwale. "Grab on and pull."

She grasped the edge of the boat first with one hand and then the other, looking at him angrily all the while, intending to pull with all her strength and rip herself in half just to prove to him that what he was asking her to do was impossible.

She gave a pull, and to her surprise, she slid free as if nothing held her. In three seconds she was in the skiff. Austin turned the motor, and the boat plowed toward shore.

Wanda looked back at the shark. It was crushing in its jaws a life-size rubber sex doll. As it thrashed and pulled the doll under, Wanda saw the face. It wasn't her. It was Shana, the girl Dirk had taken out the other night.

The water clouded with blood, and then the fin came up and headed out to sea where thousands of latex women bobbed in the waves awaiting the slithering predator.

Wanda checked herself for bite marks. Her body was riddled with them. Her torso and stomach, arms and legs and breasts and heart.

"Those will fade," Austin said.

She was ashamed to be naked in front of him.

"There's nothing to hide," he said. "I've already seen everything. I saw it all from the beginning. From the first time we talked. I drew a picture, remember? Of you."

The shore was just ahead.

31

"BEACH WEEK!"

The scratchy amplified voice was so loud she practically leapt off the couch.

"Jesus Christ, Dirk, don't point that thing at me!" It was the bullhorn he used each year on the third day of class, when he led his freshman writing class on a tour of the campus. It saved him having to shout as he pointed out the buildings and landmarks they would have to describe in their essays.

"And put some clothes on," Wanda added as she sat up.

"BUT WE DIDN'T FINISH LAST NIGHT!"

She yanked the bullhorn from his hands and threw it on a chair.

"Seriously," Dirk said. "My balls ache like hell."

"You can *go* to hell." Wanda stepped past him and went into the bathroom.

"Cook some breakfast," Dirk said outside the door. "I'll pack the car."

She waited until she heard him go upstairs. Then she used the toilet and washed up.

She listened at the door before she came out. If he was around, she'd hear him. He was always the loudest presence in the building. Any building.

She heard him thumping and thrashing in the bathroom overhead. If a normal person were making that much noise, she'd assume he was grappling with an intruder. Dirk, she guessed (correctly), was just brushing his teeth.

Famished from her long night of wandering, Wanda opened the fridge in search of breakfast.

Two eggs would be perfect, and she could warm the bacon in the microwave. Pancakes were too much work. Toast would do. And she would need coffee to shake off her sluggishness.

As she removed the eggs she told herself she might as well cook all six. And heat all the bacon, not just three strips. And make enough toast and coffee for him too. No sense in picking an unnecessary fight, which is what she'd be doing if she cooked only for herself. And, she told herself, he's easier to manage when his stomach is full.

She decided to make the pancakes too.

At breakfast, she listened to his lips smack as he ate, and she was grateful for an hour of calm, an hour without argument.

This is how it starts, she thought. This is us come full circle.

Dirk wore a bright yellow Hawaiian shirt printed with gaudy palms and hula girls.

He's already in costume, she told herself.

The giant white napkin he had tucked into his collar to keep the bacon grease off the hula girls reminded her of a baby's bib. She had told him once when he was drunk that if he wore a diaper, he wouldn't have to get up and go to the bathroom after each beer. At the time, he thought it was a great idea. He went to the grocery for more beer and a box of adult diapers, but when he tested them, he found they were only suitable for leaks and minor accidents, not the torrents he unleashed after consuming an entire twelve-pack. Wanda had to buy new couch cushions, which she'd been wanting to do anyway.

This suddenly struck her as odd. No matter how offensive his actions, she thought, I always tell myself there's something in it for me. If Peter Pennypacker peed on the couch, Louise would never let him hear the end of it. Dirk does it, and I tell myself I'm lucky because now I have an excuse to replace the cushions.

It's not just my emotional wiring that's off. It's my whole brain. Before she could proceed any further down this path of enlightenment—

"GREAT BREAKFAST!" Dirk shouted through the bullhorn.

"Put that goddamn thing away!"

"YOU GOT IT, BABE!"

He put it in the giant tote bag with the towels and sunscreen.

"You're not taking that to the beach, are you?"

"Someone has to yell at the swimmers who go out too far."

"That's the lifeguard's job," Wanda said.

"And obviously they're not doing it, or those people wouldn't be out there."

"Leave the bullhorn, Dirk. Seriously."

"Do you really want it to be on your conscience when someone drowns?"

She rolled her eyes and picked up the dishes, hers and his, before she stopped to notice what she was doing.

A few minutes later, as Dirk thumped violently in the bathroom upstairs (nose hair trim, Wanda told herself), she found her phone and called Austin.

"Hey." She sounded sheepish. "I'm sorry about last night."

"When are you guys leaving for the beach?"

"I don't know." Wanda looked out the front window. "Looks like Dirk has the car packed, but I haven't started on my bag. Plus, he's grooming. He'll be at the eyebrows next. I can't see us leaving in less than an hour."

"I'll come by."

"I'm surprised you still want to talk to me."

"You know I do."

"Well it's nice of you. To come over and say goodbye."

"I'll see you soon," he said. "But we're not saying goodbye."

32

"Did you pack the sunscreen?" Dirk asked.

She was in the bathroom packing her toothbrush and toothpaste. They didn't share a tube because she didn't squeeze from the bottom, and her tube always had a gummy crust around the opening that inspired Dirk to lecture her about how personal decline begins with minor acts of carelessness. It was she who suggested separate tubes, mainly to stop the lectures. After that, he found new things to sermonize about, to edify and improve her, for such was his love.

Wanda's shoulders tensed. "I thought you packed the sunscreen."

"Ha!" He grinned his big white smile and pointed his index finger at her. "Gotcha!"

Of course you packed it, she thought. Because once I packed it and it spilled on the towels, and that was the end of me ever packing sunscreen again.

He gave her a sudden, unwanted kiss, a quick peck on the lips. The way his face came at her, so quick and unexpected, made her jerk her head back, like a boxer trying to avoid an opponent's jab.

"Car's all packed," he said as he unzipped and peed into the toilet behind her.

"Do you have to do that while I'm in here?"

"Do you have to be in the bathroom while I pee?" His tone was light and flirty, which made his remark sound all the more rude.

She dropped her toothpaste into her bag and thought of the joint on the nightstand. If he's going to be like this for the whole two-hour drive...

But no. Austin would be by in a few minutes, and she wanted to have a clear head when they said goodbye. No joint yet. Save it for the road.

She tossed the bag of toiletries into her suitcase. She normally would pack a large suitcase for a week-long trip, but she knew that at the beach she'd wear the same clothes over and over. A few swimsuits, shorts, t-shirts, one dress, and a sweatshirt in case it got cold at night. She packed it all into one of those rolling bags that fits in an overhead bin.

"You ready?" Dirk asked.

She saw the big handprints on his pants. Pee and then wash and then ignore the hand towel that's right in front of your stupid annoying face and wipe your hands on your goddamn pants. Why are you such an ass?

Normally she would have said that aloud. But today she didn't, and she had the strange sense Dirk was disappointed in her for not snapping at him.

Why am I so irritable today, she wondered. It must be the emotional hangover from last night's fight. But today I'm doing well. I'm self-aware. I'm in control. I'm not letting us fall into the same old pattern.

Still, she couldn't resist needling him. It just slipped out. "You sure the car's packed just right?" Her voice had the taunting edge that she knew would set him off.

Dirk looked uncertain. "Yeah. Why? Do you know something I don't know?"

"I know you usually repack it three times before we leave, and today you haven't repacked at all."

Dirk looked suspicious. "What if it doesn't need repacking?"

"What if it does?"

Dirk stared at her for a few seconds, waiting for her to crack. Then he blinked. "Fuck!"

He thundered down the wooden stairs and in a minute, he was ripping everything out of the car.

Wanda heard him say hello to Austin on the sidewalk.

Austin wasn't the mushy type, or the type to draw out a long goodbye. She would greet him with a bittersweet smile, maybe a hug, and she would hide her sadness at his leaving, at her losing the one person she could truly talk to.

She zipped her bag and said to herself, "Time to close this chapter."

33

He stood with his hips against the side of his car, the way Dirk's date had stood waiting the other night. She was surprised he didn't come up the walk to meet her.

His car was packed. Judging by the way the rear of it sagged, the trunk must have been full. The back seat was crammed with boxes.

He made no motion of greeting as she approached, but his eyes were fixed on her, his expression serious.

She put her suitcase down on the sidewalk, along with the shoulder bag containing her laptop.

"You gonna do some writing at the beach?"

His tone was surprisingly cool and reserved.

"I was planning on it," Wanda said. "Listen, I'm sorry about last night."

"I'm not."

"No? You look upset." She pointed to the boxes in the back seat. "You leaving? Today? I thought it was tomorrow."

Austin shrugged. "There's no point in me being here anymore."

In the moment of awkward silence that followed, they heard Dirk curse at the open trunk of the BMW two-seater convertible just up the street.

They both turned to see him stomping down the sidewalk.

"Wandaaa!"

"What, Dirk?"

"How big is that bag?"

"This big." She pointed to the suitcase beside her.

"Why did you choose that one?" The exasperation in his tone suggested she had wronged him. "It's too big for the trunk."

"Well why'd you have to put all that crap in there?"

"Excuse me?" he said with an exaggerated tone of offense. "We're going to the beach. THE. BEACH." He let out a sigh of exasperation that said talking to idiots like her was pointless. Then he announced he was thirsty, as if that were the news the whole neighborhood had been dying to hear. He dashed up the walk and thundered across the porch and through the door, which closed behind him with a jolting slam.

Wanda let out the breath she had been holding and turned her attention back to Austin.

"Are you really going with him?" Austin asked.

"Of course I am. Where else would I go?" She noticed then that his front passenger seat was empty. The whole front of the car was immaculate, as if prepared to receive her.

"Oh, come on, Austin!"

"How many times have you asked yourself that question?" His face had a look of immovable resolve.

"What question?"

"*Where else would I go?*" He could see her getting uncomfortable, so he pressed his point. "How many times, Wanda? Isn't that always your excuse for not leaving him?"

"Austin, this isn't the time."

"Every day since you've been with him hasn't been the time. But someday has to be the time. Someday you have to do it."

She shook her head. "Not today, Austin."

"I don't understand what holds you."

"No," she said, her anger rising. "No, you don't. And Louise doesn't either. And neither does Audrey. But you all judge. All of you judge what you don't understand."

"But you're good with it?" Austin asked.

Dirk exploded through the door of the house with his bullhorn.

"WANDAAA!"

With his toy in his hand, his magical Dirk amplifier, he was as happy as a kindergartener on the last day of school.

On his way past them, Dirk told Wanda to get in the car and told Austin to have a nice trip. Then he was back at the BMW, slamming the trunk. He turned and said through the bullhorn, "YOU'LL HAVE TO PUT YOUR BAG IN YOUR LAP."

He grinned at the sound of his voice filling the neighborhood. Then, like a boy just discovering the pleasures of touching himself, he had to do it again.

"I'LL BE IN THE CAR!"

The curtain in the house across the street opened so the neighbor could look out on the commotion.

"You're good waking up to that?" Austin asked. "Day after day?"

God, he's so persistent. "Drop it, Austin."

"Tomorrow and tomorrow and tomorrow…"

Those words sent a jolt through her. How did he know to say that?

"Austin, what you did last night was nice. I mean, it was a big fuck-you to Dirk—"

"It was."

"—and I liked the kiss more than I thought I would, but... You're not, like, my knight in shining armor. I mean, I like you, but please don't have any delusions about—"

"This isn't a seduction, Wanda. It's an intervention."

Why did those words shake her so?

"You know, I tried to get Audrey here. I tried to get Louise and Peter."

"Oh, that would have backfired," Wanda said. "Audrey maybe, but not the other two. I'd do the opposite of whatever they said."

"That's exactly it," Austin said.

"WANDAAAA!" Dirk had opened the roof of the convertible and pointed the bullhorn to the sky. "OH WANDA WIIIIIILEY! YOUR VACATION IS WAITING!"

"That's exactly your problem," Austin said. "You think it's all about seduction and passion and drama. But it's not. Real life is written in prose. It's practical and sometimes it's boring. It's what you see when you look at me. Your problem is that you're addicted to drama. You're scared that if you lose the violent ups and downs you won't be able to write anymore. You'll fall out of touch with passion and not be able to lay it out on the page for your readers. But how much is it costing you? How much is this life costing you?"

"Damnit, Austin!" She was angry now that he had poked his intrusive finger directly into the heart of the matter. "There are things you will never understand, because you're not that kind of person. There are things you can't even know you don't understand."

"Like what? That he reads you? That he sees into you and always knows what you're feeling?"

"Yes, for starters."

"Of course he knows your feelings. He's the one who puts them there in the first place. He knows your insecurities because he's always stoking them. He knows when you're desperate for attention and approval, because he made you that way. All his words and actions are calculated to make you dependent. And then when he gives you what you want, you think it's the greatest thing in the world, because you've been so deprived. You've wanted it so badly you're like a starving animal rejoicing over a morsel of food."

"How dare you talk to me that way!" His words were too much on the mark. She didn't want to cry. She was humiliated enough as it was. "What the hell do you want from me anyway?"

"I want you to leave with me. Now."

She laughed scornfully. "I'm not in love with you."

"I know that, Wanda."

She was surprised that bounced right off him. She had intended it to hurt.

"What's my angle?" Austin asked rhetorically. "Is that what you're wondering?"

Why could he see what she was thinking when she couldn't see what he was thinking? Her position of powerlessness made her even more angry.

"My angle is I think you're a beautiful person. I told you that. And I think he's horrible. And I can't stand to see someone like you dominated by someone like him. I can't just walk away from that and let it happen. The world where things like that are allowed to happen is a dark and bitter world. That's not the world I want to live in. That's not the world I want you to live in."

His words had caught her off guard, as did the intensity of his conviction.

"WAN…" There was the pause. She winced in anticipation of the coming syllable. "DAAAAAAAAAAA!"

She balled her fists and screamed, "Shut up, Dirk!"

"BEACH WEEK!"

Austin put his hand on her shoulder. She didn't want to look at him or hear any more of his words.

"Did Dirk open the gift? The one I brought over last night?"

"I don't know."

"You would know if he did. Go inside and open it."

She hesitated, wondering what this new ploy was about.

"I don't even know where he put it," Wanda said.

"Well then think. Where would Dirk put a gift addressed to Dirk?"

"On his desk?"

"Go open it and look," Austin said. "And then make your decision. Pick which car you want to get into."

She tried to read his face to see what he was up to.

"Go," he said.

34

"There's a lot of shouting going on up there," Trevor said.

"I can see it right out here," Hannah replied. She pointed at the roiling black smoke beyond the rattling windows. "Everything is getting churned up from the depths."

Trevor stood by the mantle of the empty fireplace and watched her. She reclined on the couch in her black slacks and white blouse, puzzling through the Rubik's cube. She had four sides of it solved already.

"You know what it is?" Hannah looked up at Trevor. "That gets to her?"

"What?"

"It's the words. She's always been susceptible to words. Her writing. Her love of Shakespeare. Some people respond to music and some to touch. For her it's language. There's a direct line into her mind and heart, and Austin knows that. He knows exactly what to say."

"You're awfully calm," Trevor said.

"The end is near."

"What do you want to do when you get out of here?"

She sat up and resumed her work on the puzzle. "I've thought about that. I've had years to think about it, but I don't like to get my hopes up. She's so out of touch with herself, I fear another letdown. Like she'll try to write me into another romance where I just don't fit. I don't want to be in a romance."

"What do you want?"

She put the cube down on the couch beside her. "You'll think it's funny," she said.

"Try me."

"I want to be in politics. And I don't mean the local school board. I mean the big time."

"Be careful what you wish for," Trevor said.

"Why do you say that?"

"I've spent time guarding presidents and senators. Those jobs aren't easy. In fact, they're maddening."

"But what qualities does a person need to do them?" Hannah stood and walked toward him, as if to challenge him. "Vision, compassion, leadership. A strong practical streak. A focus on results. I have those qualities."

"You forgot ego and a thick skin," Trevor said.

"You don't need a thick skin if you don't have a big ego."

"Maybe so. But for every friend you make in politics, you'll get an enemy."

Hannah shrugged.

"The worst thing," Trevor said, "is that you have to compromise all the time, and when you do, you lie awake at night thinking about the people you just sold out in order to get that compromise. The politicians who really care— and there are some who really do—they're always aware of the price they've paid. They're always thinking how far they've fallen short of serving everyone they wanted to serve, of solving all the problems they wanted to solve."

"Well that's the price of compassion, isn't it? Feeling the pain of those left behind. But what's a leader without that? What's a life without compassion?"

She turned and paced toward the far side of the room.

"I still want to do it," she said.

"I can see that."

"I mean, when you feel you were put here to do something, you have to be given the chance to do it. Otherwise, you haven't lived. And there's a sadness to that. A sadness Wanda feels, and I feel. My worry is that she'll never give me the chance."

She walked back and stood beside him by the cold fireplace. "Do you think you could ask her?"

Trevor shook his head. "You need to ask her."

"She never hears me."

Trevor went to the couch and picked up the cube.

"You need to ask her," he repeated. "This is between you two."

He handed her the puzzle.

35

Wanda made her way slowly up the steps to the porch, her heart swelling with fear. Dirk had left the door unlocked. Just like him. Going away for a week and leaving the house open.

She walked inside and up the stairs. Everything had a sudden clarity. A frightful clarity and presence. The grain of the wood on the bannister, the brightness of the late morning light spilling from the bedroom. The echo of her footsteps in the empty house reminded her of the day six years ago when they had found this place, when he stood talking in the kitchen with the realtor—flirting with the realtor—while Wanda walked the floors upstairs and mentally placed the furniture in the room of the child she would give him. In the room that was now his office.

There on the desk sat the package, wrapped in green. She picked it up and felt the frame. A photo, she thought.

She opened the little card taped to the front.

To Dirk. From Wanda.

Why from Wanda, she wondered.

She opened the taped seam along the back, careful not to rip it. She unfolded the paper and looked at the frame, afraid to turn it over.

I don't want to cry anymore, she thought. This better not make me cry. I don't want to walk past Austin all red-faced and puffy-eyed and admit that I'm a coward. Why did he have to turn this into such a scene?

She turned the frame over. There was no photo, only words. Fourteen lines, carefully transcribed.

She read them once, straight through, and they struck like thunder, giving voice with eloquent power to what she already knew and understood. No one could have stated more clearly the feelings she had worked so hard to suppress. For several minutes, she sat still and quiet with her eyes closed, letting the words sink in.

She lay the frame face-down in the wrapping, folded the paper, and re-taped the seam. She turned the package face-up and left it there with the card on top.

To Dirk. From Wanda.

She didn't lock the house on the way out.

Austin sat in his car, the engine idling as he watched.

She opened the passenger door, threw her bags on the floor, and got in.

"Drive," she said.

"You OK?"

"I'm OK."

It wasn't just clarity she had now. It was certainty and resolve. An unshakable resolve that he could see. That gave him hope, because he knew that if he could pull the two magnets far enough apart, they would lose their hold on each other.

He pulled out to the street, past Dirk in the BMW.

"We're going all the way across the country," Austin said.

"I know." She looked straight ahead and her tone was flat.

"It's a long drive."

"The farther the better."

Dirk caught on as they neared the end of the block. He put the BMW in gear and lurched into the driving lane. At the intersection, he stopped behind them.

"WANDAAA! YOU'RE IN THE WRONG CAR!"

He didn't get it. This was just another day, another fight, and his yo-yo would come back to him like it always did.

Austin turned the corner, onto the boulevard that led to the highway that led to the other side of the country and a life that wouldn't be this one anymore.

In the left lane he picked up speed.

"How did you know?" she asked.

"I know you, Wanda."

Dirk pulled up alongside them on the right and pointed the bullhorn out the driver's window.

"WANDAAAAA!"

She winced and put her hand to her ear.

"Watch where you're going, Dirk!"

"WAN—"

He slammed into the back of a parked police cruiser before he could get the last syllable out.

To the last syllable of recorded time.

She turned to see the wreck. The airbag had exploded into his face while he held the bullhorn.

"I hope he didn't knock his pretty teeth out." She faced forward again. "They're so important to him."

Austin shrugged.

"Seriously, Austin, how did you know?"

"Everyone knew."

"No, not that. I mean the words. How did you know those would be the words?"

"I listen to you, Wanda." He kept his eyes on the road ahead. "I've listened to every word you've ever said. Even when you weren't listening to yourself."

36

"You've been around a lot," Hannah said. "You've seen much more of the world than I have."

"I've seen the bad parts of it," Trevor replied. "The politics, the warring ideologies, the killing."

They were sitting side by side on the couch. The house was growing lighter. Beyond the parted curtains, a powerful wind pushed the fog away until at last a stream of sunlight poured in.

"If I were ever to go into politics," she said, "it would be nice to have someone to bounce ideas off. Someone whose perspective is different from mine. Someone who can listen long enough to get me, who can call me out when I'm wrong and reaffirm me when I'm right."

Why is she prettier now, Trevor wondered, in those plain black slacks than she had been in her satin dress? How strange, he thought, to be so drawn to a woman he had never even mentally undressed. It seemed an impossibly long time ago that he had thought she was a witch. How had she come to this?

His conversation with the president came back to him. The tough-guy president, his former CO and brother in arms, who had willingly crossed the street from fame and power to anonymity and quiet contemplation.

"You ever watch the sparrows hop around and pick at crumbs on the sidewalk?"

"That would bore the shit out of me."

"That's what I used to think.... I'm beginning to understand why the Buddha sat still to find enlightenment. I used to think it was something you had to go out and grab by the balls."

How had Hannah come to look different from all other women, Trevor wondered. What dimension existed in this relationship that was missing from all the others?

"Respect," Hannah whispered. "It's the cornerstone of everything."

She kissed his cheek, and when she stood, she handed him the puzzle.

All six sides were solved.

37

With each passing hour on the open highway, Wanda breathed more freely. The fifteen hundred miles between the Atlantic and the Rockies were one big cornfield interspersed here and there with patches of soybeans, shopping malls, and car dealerships.

All my heroines, she thought, trod a well-known path that was preordained by the rules of the genre. The path of a single destiny, of one right fate, and the challenge was simply to secure it. Or let it secure them.

But the future now is as open-ended as these plains. A person could go for a thousand miles in any direction, and still the horizon would be impossibly far off. Still there would be no end to reach. A journey rather than an arrival.

She looked at Austin as he drove, and she thought, He asks so little of the world. Nothing, almost. He finds contentment in what's before him.

He doesn't poke at my emotions the way Dirk did. He doesn't need the constant reassurance that he still has a hold on me. He simply lets me be.

In the past, she would have interpreted that as indifference or neglect. When Dirk ignored her, she picked at him, just to make sure she still mattered. The ebb and flow of Dirk and Wanda were tides on a sea of insecurity. There had been no nurturing or growth, only the avoidance of what they feared would be the deeper loss of not having each other to abuse.

On the third night of the trip, on the plains of eastern Colorado, when she and Austin were still sleeping in separate beds, she dreamed of Hannah.

Hannah approached her on a flat country road between rippling fields of wheat. She wore the white muslin dress of an 1890's farm maiden. Wanda worried Hannah would be angry. Before Hannah could speak, she said, "I know I've neglected you. I know I've let you down."

"You didn't let me down. You just didn't listen. Take me out of this dress, will you?"

"What do you want to wear?" Wanda asked.

"What do *you* want to wear?"

Faded jeans and an oversized t-shirt. Soft cotton all around.

"That's better," Hannah said, spreading her arms and looking at the baggy shirt sleeves. "I never wanted to be your heroine."

"I know."

They walked side by side toward the mountains in the west.

"I'm more outward looking. I want to make a difference in the world."

"I know," said Wanda.

"I need a bigger stage."

"I know."

"Then why did you write me like that? Like my destiny was to be someone's girlfriend?"

"Because that's how all the stories are. That's what people know and respond to."

"You could write a different story."

"Maybe," said Wanda. "But I don't know if people would buy it."

"Try," said Hannah.

They had come to a stop at the foot of the mountains, the mountains that had been a hundred miles off just a minute earlier.

"How did we get here?" Wanda asked.

Hannah pointed to the towering summits and said, "Try."

38
Eighteen Months Later

Dirk Jaworski sat at his desk facing the monitor with the same open document he'd been staring at for years. The lonely letter X stared back at him. He hadn't touched the half-empty tequila bottle beside the keyboard since last night. Or was it the night before?

The empty beer bottles on the bookshelves told visitors what had caused him to lose his shape and make his fat bottom meld into his chair the way Wanda's had once melded into hers.

What comes after X, Dirk wondered. Goddamnit, something has to!

Xylophone!

Yes, he thought. Exclamation point and all!

This was a breakthrough.

He had added eight letters to his masterwork. The first letter had taken four years. And now, in a blinding flash of inspiration, eight more had come all at once. If one letter was four years of work, then eight was...

Dirk opened the calculator application and typed in the numbers.

8 x 4 = 32

Thirty-two years of work in a single morning!

You see, he told himself. You see now what a drag she was on your creativity, with her neediness and her complaints. She was an anchor around your neck. Now she's someone else's problem. Now she's with Austin. Or who knows, maybe she ran out on him too.

Thirty-two years of work in a single day deserved a reward. He poured a shot of tequila and swished it in the glass and thought about the interview he'd seen an hour earlier. Wanda on that morning TV show, all healthy and aglow, all smiles and clear skin and eager answers.

For Christ's sake, Dirk thought, she's pushing books on television.

He drank the shot.

Television! That bastion of illiteracy! So what if she sold half a million copies in the first two months? There are over three hundred million fools in this country—football fans and wrestling fans and people who think Katy Perry can sing—and so what if she sold half a million books? She captures a fraction of a percent of that sea of idiots, and for that they celebrate her and put her on TV?

He poured another shot.

"Now you admit you failed on the Trevor Dunwoody book," said the interviewer, a middle-aged woman in a knee-length skirt.

Wanda smiled and gave a big thumbs down. "Oh, I bombed it. I totally bombed it."

"Not your kind of story?"

Wanda shook her head. "Not my kind of story. Not my kind of character."

"And that hurt your career," said the interviewer.

"Well, the editor was angry. No, the editor was irate. Because I had Trevor solving problems through diplomacy."

"It was the only novel where he didn't have a love interest," the interviewer noted.

"Or use his gun."

"What were you thinking?" the interviewer asked with a laugh.

Wanda laughed too. "I was thinking the genre needed a reboot."

"So Ed Parsippany's editor fired you."

"Yup."

"And then you had a falling out with your own editor."

"And my agent," said Wanda. "She wanted another romance. She wanted the tried and true formula with guaranteed sales."

"But you tried to pitch her something different?"

"Nomance." Wanda made air quotes around the word.

"What is nomance?"

"Fulfillment not in the shape of a penis. Wait, can I say that on TV?"

"You just did. But Hannah Sharpe," said the interviewer, "Senator Sharpe, she does have a man in her life."

"She does. But he's not the story. *They* are not the story. It's the story of a woman with moral vision and courage and the ability to rally people. It's the story of a woman who has tremendous common sense, who helps others to see clearly and move forward toward a better world. She inspires people to act."

"And where did you come up with the character of her husband? He's an unusually supportive, enlightened character."

"Willy? He came of my experience writing the Dunwoody book. Willy is basically the anti-Trevor."

"And, I'm sorry, I just have to ask." The interviewer leaned forward with a smile and tapped her knee. "The name? Willy Keeper. Where did that come from?"

"Oh..." Wanda waved off the question, laughing inwardly at her memory of the prayer Trevor uttered that night in Lafayette Park. "Long story."

"Now your agent didn't want this book, is that right?"

"Oh, no," said Wanda. "Romance sells. Nomance is... an unknown quantity."

"So you self-published."

"I did." Wanda nodded. She was smiling.

"Why do you think the book took off the way it did?"

She threw her arms up as if to say she had no idea. "Timing, I suppose. I guess it just hit a nerve."

She hadn't been stoned in eighteen months. She no longer needed to medicate herself to tolerate her day-to-day life, and when she stopped smoking, she stopped craving sweets. She went back to eating the healthy foods she had once naturally preferred. Her energy returned and she became active again.

Dirk couldn't conceive of the change that had come over her, much less give her credit for it. He had decided her healthy appearance was due to good makeup and lighting. Her confidence and energy, he was sure, came from being the center of attention. He knew what it was like to have all eyes on him. It puffed him up like a big colorful balloon.

What he missed most since the loss of his professorship was the auditorium, being at the front of the lecture hall filled with young women. There were young men there too, to fill out the crowd, but in Dirk's mind, only the women mattered.

Shana, the dark-haired one who had waited outside the house that evening when Wanda was cooking lobster,

Shana was his downfall. If it weren't for her stupidity and carelessness, he'd still have his job. He had convinced her that a condom would deprive her of the full Dirk Jaworski experience, that skin on skin would be immeasurably better than that sensation-deadening bag.

And then she had gotten pregnant. Of all the stupid things to do!

When she complained to the university, two more women came forward.

At the hearing, Dirk was confident he'd be put on leave and brought back in a year, after the controversy had blown over. But that wasn't how it went.

"Three women have come forward," said the dean, who was herself a woman. "That means there might be ten."

Dirk was secretly pleased that she gave him credit for seducing ten women. The number was actually higher, but this wasn't the time to correct her.

"The university has a duty not only to educate but to protect. There is no place for you here."

Dirk was sure he could get a job at another university, but the blot on his record made him untouchable.

His new position, bagging groceries at the supermarket, didn't bestow the same aura of power as his professorship. He had no stage to strut on, no ready-made crowd to hang on his words. The women in the checkout line passed too quickly for him to impress with one of his carefully crafted performances. Some of them were old and not worth talking to. The young ones told him what to do, where not to put the eggs and how not to crush the bread.

Finding new partners was now infinitely harder than it used to be. They weren't his students so he didn't know their names. He only knew them by their attributes. The blue-eyed blonde at the coffee shop with the perky tits. She had laughed at two of his jokes. One laugh could have been written off as luck, but two? Two meant the door was open.

And then there was the brunette in the dentist's office who was so plainly insecure, so pathetically eager to please. Sure, she was fat, but her weakness cried out for a savior, for a dashing, glorious Prince Charming to lift her up... And to remind her every now and then how lucky she was to have him, what a nothing she had been before he discovered her.

As he poured another shot and admired his budding masterpiece on the computer monitor, Wanda sat in the back of a cab in New York City, heading to a second interview.

What a difference, she thought, to have someone who gets you. Who appreciates you, who lets you be you. Kindness and decency are worth more than passion in the long run. What an utterly different world I live in today.

Her notion of love now was thoroughly unromantic. It was like food or water or shelter—things which, when they are consistently and reliably present, provide the foundation of a healthy life. To obsess over them was unhealthy. To pursue them single-mindedly was to live an unbalanced existence.

There were still moments when she missed the intensity of the destructive passion she had shared with Jerk, as she now called him. But when she missed the intense highs and lows, she reminded herself how predictable those days had been. How all the same, how like the hamster's wheel, running and running to feel you were alive but never getting anywhere. Exhausted all the time.

In six and a half years with Dirk, all the yesterdays had been the same. Today, in this cab in New York, her life was a million miles from where it had been the day she walked out on him. In a few minutes, she would be talking to an editor from a literary journal, the kind of journal whose editors looked down on genre fiction the way Dirk had once looked down on her. They had finally picked up one of her books. They had gotten a peek into her mind, and now they wanted a feature interview.

At his desk, Dirk considered another shot of liquor.

Too early, he thought. Better switch to beer.

He looked at the gift that had sat unopened for eighteen months. The little rectangle in green wrapping. *To Dirk, from Wanda.*

All right, Wanda, since today seems to be your day...

He picked it up and tore recklessly at the taped seam. A frame, he thought. A photo of Wanda and me? Do I really want to see it?

He turned it over and read the sonnet.

My love is as a fever, longing still
For that which longer nurseth the disease,
Feeding on that which doth preserve the ill,
Th' uncertain sickly appetite to please.
My reason, the physician to my love,
Angry that his prescriptions are not kept,
Hath left me, and I desperate now approve
Desire is death, which physic did except.
Past cure I am, now reason is past care,
And frantic-mad with evermore unrest;
My thoughts and my discourse as madmen's are,
At random from the truth, vainly expressed:
    For I have sworn thee fair, and thought thee bright,
    Who art as black as hell, as dark as night.

"You dumb bitch," he muttered. "You got the commas wrong."

He reached for his red professor's pen and began marking up the text, happy to have been given the opportunity, one last time, to show her who was right.

ABOUT THE AUTHOR

Andrew Diamond writes mystery, crime, noir, and comedy. His books feature cinematic prose, strong characterization, twisting plots, and dark humor.

You can find Andrew on Amazon, Goodreads, and Facebook, and at https://adiamond.me.

ACKNOWLEDGMENTS

Thank you, Lindsay Heider Diamond, for another excellent cover. And thanks to Meredith Tennant for proofreading.

TO HELL WITH JOHNNY MANIC

John Manis, aka Johnny Manic—charming, stylish, impulsive, and reckless—is racked with guilt over the secret he doesn't dare tell. Marilyn Dupree, passionate and volatile, has too much money and the wrong husband. Johnny and Marilyn have a chemistry like nitrogen and glycerine, and that makes Detective Lou Eisenfall very uneasy.

"Poor Lou," Johnny observes as his mind begins to unravel. "There's a madman running around his town, and who knows what he'll do next?"

A twisting tale of deception, murder, and psychological suspense, Johnny Manic is a throwback to the classic crime fiction of Raymond Chandler and Jim Thompson, with overtones of the multilayered *Fight Club* and *Gone Girl*.

"A feverishly readable psychological noir." - Kirkus Reviews

"A truly riveting tale of deception, murder and psychological suspense. One of the year's best thrillers." - BestThrillers.com

GATE 76

A mysterious woman fleeing an unknown terror boards the wrong plane at San Francisco International and disappears into the heart of the country. Freddy Ferguson, a troubled detective with a violent past, believes she's the last living witness to a crime that has captivated the nation.

Sifting through the wreckage of her past, he begins to understand who she's running from, and why. Now he must track her down before her pursuers can silence her for good.

A modern crime thriller with elements of Raymond Chandler and the classic pulp mysteries of the 1950's, Gate 76 weaves a deeply personal tale of witness and investigator, loss and redemption.

Named to Kirkus Reviews' Best Books of 2018

"A consummate thriller with some of the best characterization you'll see all year." - Kirkus Reviews (starred review)

"One of the year's best thrillers." - BestThrillers.com

IMPALA

After four years on the straight and narrow, Russell Fitzpatrick has a boring job, the wrong woman, and an itch for something more. All he needs to get his life going again is a nudge in the wrong direction.

When he receives a cryptic email from a legendary and slightly deranged fellow hacker—his old friend, Charlie, whom he knows to be dead—he tries to tell himself it's none of his concern. But the guy who stalks him across town at night, the two thugs waiting in the alley, and a ruthless FBI agent let him know his days are numbered if he doesn't turn over the money Charlie stole.

The problem is, Russ doesn't have it. As his enemies close in from all sides, Russ slowly unwinds the mystery of his old friend's paranoid mind and finds that Charlie left behind something worth much more than the money. And no one but him is onto it...

An Amazon Best Book of the Month - Sept. 2016 - Mystery/Thriller

An IndieReader Best of 2016 Selection

Gold Medal Winner - 2017 Readers' Favorite Awards

First Place Winner - Genre Fiction - 24th Annual Writer's Digest Awards

WARREN LANE

Susan Moore is about to hire the wrong man to investigate her philandering husband, Will. There's something not quite right about that detective, but he's all she has at the moment. "Warren Lane" drinks too much and has a hard time staying out of trouble. He's just the kind of guy Will's mistress can't resist. And everyone is starting to figure out that Will is hiding a lot more than his affair with a reckless young woman.

With a bit of mystery, romance, crime, and suspense, Warren Lane has his hands full in this dark comedy of errors.

"A quirky, intriguing and wholly original read... beautifully written and expertly plotted." — Readers' Favorite (5 stars)